Andy Catlett

Also by Wendell Berry

WENDELL BERRY

Andy Catlett: Early Travels

A Novel

Shoemaker & Hoard

Library of Congress Cataloging-in-Publication Data
Berry, Wendell, 1934–
   Andy Catlett : early travels / Wendell Berry.
      p. cm.
   ISBN-13: 978-1-59376-136-3
   ISBN-10: 1-59376-136-8
1. Port William (Ky. : Imaginary place)—Fiction. 2. Boys—Fiction.
3. Grandparent and child—Fiction. 4. Kentucky—Fiction. 5. Christmas stories. I. Title.

PS3552.E75A85 2007
813'.54—DC22

2006030687

Book design by David Bullen
Map and genealogy designed by Molly O'Halloran
Genealogy prepared by David S. McCowen

Printed in the United States of America

Shoemaker & Hoard

An Imprint of Avalon Publishing Group, Inc.
1400 65th Street, Suite 250
Emeryville, CA 94608
AVALON
publishing group incorporated   Distributed by Publishers Group West

10 9 8 7 6 5 4 3 2 1

To the grandchildren,
mine and everybody's

I

It was still way in the night, as it seemed to me, when my father woke me by gently shaking my shoulder with his hand.

I said aloud, "No. Wait!" in a dream I was having, and then, "What?"

"Get up, honey. I've about got your breakfast ready."

Ordinarily the news that my father was cooking my breakfast would have made me cover my head. He cooked with what I thought an unseemly haste and show of force, like a man putting out a fire. You wouldn't have been surprised to see him lean over and blow on the coils of our then fairly new electric stove.

But he was in one of his finer moods, as I could tell by the touch of his hand, and I promptly remembered that this was the day of my trip to Port William.

"Be quiet, now. The others are still asleep," he said, and he went out so quietly he seemed almost not to have been there.

"Maybe I'm dreaming," I thought, but by the light coming in from the hall I could see my brother, Henry, curled up beneath the covers, deeply asleep in his bed. And then a thrill of pleasure came upon me. I felt in the shadow of my own bed to make sure of my small grip, packed with my clothes, toothbrush, and my new copy of Sidney Lanier's *The Boy's King Arthur*, imbued already with the voice of my mother, raptly reading it to me. It was still there. I got up then, dressed in a hurry in the shadowy room, picked up my grip, and went quietly out the door.

It was the fourth day after Christmas, 1943, and I was nine years old. Port William, the native community of both my parents, was all of ten miles from our house in Hargrave. It was in fact my own native community. I had been born there, had been there hundreds of times, sometimes to stay weeks at a stretch with my Feltner grandparents, my mother's parents, in the town of Port William itself, or with my Catlett grandparents out on the Bird's Branch road. But this time it was going to be different. This time I was going on the bus by myself, alone. It was going to be an adventure, as my parents saw it, a new experience that I would greatly enjoy. As I saw it, it was nothing less than my first step into manhood.

How this had come about I no longer remember and cannot guess. It may have been that my parents were giving a New Year's Eve party at our house, or were going to one elsewhere, and were distributing us children here and there ahead of time, starting with me, the oldest. But the sympathy that comes with age causes me to consider also the possibility that they were shipping me off for a few days just to give themselves a taste of freedom. For I had not grown, as I preferred to think, into the vaguest semblance of adulthood, but rather into a serious and lasting form of nuisancehood. As even I had noticed, I could not be good at home and at school at the same time, which meant that I was a worry to my parents all the time. At school I had become a fourth-grade Thomas Paine, striking blows for liberty, which of course earned me in return blows of yardsticks, rulers, and other pedagogical weapons, which I welcomed as distractions from the established order. At home I was actuated, like Daniel Boone, by a desire for elbow room, and our house seemed to me to be growing smaller by the day, as densely crowded by the other five members of our family as if it had been no bigger than a phone booth. And so I can't think now that my parents were grieving over my departure or that they were going to miss me much.

On the other hand, I was good, a model boy, at least when I was in sight, on my visits to both sets of my grandparents. In their houses, for me, peace reigned, and I could even count on being spoiled a little as a just compensation for my goodness. And so of course I loved those visits, especially when I could go alone.

When I got downstairs my father had my breakfast on the table: orange juice, eggs, bacon, and toast. The bacon fat had not been fried quite crisp. The eggs were done "over easy," as I liked them, but were rather crunchy around the edges because he had had the skillet too hot. And he had smeared the butter on the toast *after* he had toasted it. He certainly was not as good a cook as my mother, but I wisely made no comment.

I only said, "Where's the jelly?"

"You don't need any jelly," he said in perfect good humor, meaning, I judged, that he had not been able to find it.

"I don't reckon I do," I said.

He said, "Have you washed your face?"

"No," I said, "but I'm going to directly."

He had cleaned up his own plate and was sipping his coffee and reading the paper. He evidently had plans of his own for that early morning. He was dressed for the office and was already wearing his hat.

When I had finished eating he said, "Put your dishes in the sink."

I carried my dishes away, and when I came back he said, still reading the paper, "Go to the toilet."

I did, and when I was finished I went to the further trouble of washing my face and of wetting my hair and combing it both front and back. I didn't brush my teeth because I had packed my toothbrush the night before.

When he was ready, my father put on his overcoat and handed me my mackinaw and toboggan.

"It'll be cold out there," he said. "Have you got enough clothes?"

"Long underwear and sweater. Extra clothes in the grip."

"Where are your gloves?"

"In my coat pocket."

"Well, put on your overshoes."

I did, while he watched. He picked up the grip, and we started for the door.

"Be quiet," he said.

He had things on his mind. At the start of the morning you could feel him aiming himself into the day. We drove down into town, to Front Street, without talking. I was wide awake, and it was good to feel the earliness of the morning, the town dark yet and mostly quiet. People were just up, or still waking up, or still asleep. We passed through the pools of light from the streetlights, one after another. The sound of the car's engine was loud and then quiet, quiet and then again loud, as we went by the other cars parked here and there along the still street.

My father parked the car in front of the Poppy Shop, just a few doors down from his office. The Poppy Shop liked to call itself a "luncheonette." It opened early in the morning for breakfast, served coffee, sandwiches, ice cream, and such all day, and did duty besides as our bus station. As we got out of the car, I was quick to take charge of the grip myself. I didn't want to be seen allowing my father to carry it for me, and I didn't want there to be any mistaking who the traveler was.

When we went in, my father stepped up to where Miss Angela Davis was standing behind the cash register. Miss Angela was the proprietress of the Poppy Shop. Behind her back some of the men called her "Ample Angela." To my mother she was known as a "sweet person."

"A ticket to Port William, Miss Angela, if you please," my father said.

"Why, Wheeler, is Andy leaving home?" Miss Angela said, peeping around my father at me and my grip.

"He's pulling out," my father said.

"I know you're going to miss that boy."

"It's the truth," my father said. "Make that a round trip."

Miss Angela laughed. She handed him the ticket. He turned to me. "Here. Put this ticket in your pocket now, so you won't lose it."

"Yes, sir."

He still had his wallet in his hand. He took out a dollar bill and gave it to me. "Put this in your pocket too." And he stuck out his hand.

I understood something then: He wanted to hug me—if we had been alone he would have—but he didn't want to embarrass me.

We shook hands. "Put that money in your pocket," he said. "Be careful with it."

"Yes, sir," I said, being conscientiously polite there in public, and wishing suddenly that he *would* hug me.

"You'll be all right," he said. And then, turning to Miss Angela, he said, "He'll want to get off at the upper end of the Bird's Branch road, the Port William end."

Miss Angela, looking past him at me and smiling, said, "He won't need to worry."

And then with the instant haste that was his way, my father strode out the door.

The Poppy Shop was a small place, with a few booths and a few small tables. The chairs at the tables had round seats with backs and legs of twisted wire. There were several customers, eating breakfast or drinking coffee, getting ready to go to work.

One of the tables was empty. I put my grip on one of the chairs and sat in another.

My uncle Andrew had given me a dollar at Christmas, and so now I had two. I laid the two together, folded them up, and put them into the little coin purse I had in my pocket. I also had a nickel and a dime.

Miss Angela came over to my table. "You've got a little while to wait, honey. Do you want a cup of coffee or something?"

I said, "No, mam," but that sounded impolite. It sounded somehow ungrateful, and so I said, "Yes, mam."

"Coffee?" she said.

I said, "Yes, mam."

Though of course I had seen other people drink it, I had never tasted coffee in my life. My mother did not think it healthful for children to drink coffee. Privately, I thought coffee had an excellent smell, and I had looked forward to being old enough to drink it. And now, just because I was unaccustomed to the ways of the world and was embarrassed and wished to be polite to an older person, which would have pleased my mother, I was going to drink some coffee without being old enough.

Miss Angela set a full steaming cup in front of me. I stirred it a little, as the coffee drinkers I knew usually did, and then I took a sip from the spoon and was amazed that anything could taste so little like it smelled. The bitterness of it puckered my mouth. Miss Angela, who had been watching me, laughed in such a hearty, friendly way that I wasn't embarrassed but was merely grateful to be the cause of her amusement. Sugar was rationed because of the war, and people were encouraged to drink their coffee without it. Miss Angela, a patriot, did not supply sugar until specifically asked. But she went to the kitchen and brought back a sugar bowl, which she set down in front of me. She put two spoonsful of sugar into my cup and a generous dollop of cream.

"Now stir it," she said, "and see if it don't taste better."

I stirred it and tasted it again, and she was right. The sugar and cream made it taste more like it smelled. It only needed to be a little sweeter, and when she went away I added two more spoonsful of sugar. It went down very pleasantly after that, though I was already wondering how much my extravagance with the sugar might have hurt "the war effort." My conscience was not always alert, but when alerted it went eagerly about its duty.

When Miss Angela passed by again, she said, "How's your coffee, hon?"

"Just fine," I said. "How much do I owe you for it, please, mam?"

"You're such a nice, polite young man, I think I'll just charge it to your daddy. He's a generous fellow, isn't he?"

I couldn't have disagreed more, even though he had just given me a dollar, even though I would eventually know him as a generous man. In fact, my father had learned the lessons of the thirties pretty thoroughly, though of course I was incapable of any such insight at the age of nine. He didn't like to see money thrown away on such things as I was always needing nickels for, and so he was not especially generous with nickels. He was apt to burden me by asking, "What do you want with it?" or

"What do you need it for?" or "Do you think nickels grow on trees?" Perhaps as a result, I too grew up under the shadow of the Depression, and it is still with me. I still suspect, like many of my predecessors here in Port William, that it will come back again, and that it taught lessons that needed to be learned.

And so I didn't know what to say to Miss Angela, who proceeded to give me a small prompt: "He wouldn't mind buying a boy a cup of coffee, would he?"

I knew perfectly well that he would mind. Embarrassed again, I gave her the first grown up–sounding answer I could think of: "If it suits him, it'll tickle the hell out of me." And then I slapped my hand over my mouth.

Too late, of course. I had spoken loudly, and the place was suddenly full of laughter. For a few seconds I had a sort of vision of myself sitting there red-faced and grinning, embarrassed, scared, and proud.

The episode gave me a sort of fame, and of course my father heard of it. Two or three weeks later I happened to encounter him on the sidewalk in front of the courthouse. He was standing with his hands in the pockets of his overcoat, talking to his friend Charlie Hardy.

I gave them a wave and said, "Hi."

"That's Miss Angela's buddy, ain't it?" Mr. Hardy said.

My father snorted. "That's him." He reached into his pants pocket, drew out a nickel, and handed it to me. "Here. Go buy yourself a cup of coffee."

The war changed things. It was changing the world, and it was changing us. I didn't know it then, but sugar rationing was changing the way we would live after the war. Businesses and restaurants were given larger rations of sugar than households, and this helped to shift the dependence of households from their own kitchens to commercial bakeries. Betty Crocker was the "homemaker" who got the most sugar, and she did more and more of the baking.

Because of the war we certainly knew that history was happening to us, but it was happening to us more than we knew. History and conscience, however, did not stop me from enjoying my over-sweetened cup of coffee. I drank it to the last slow trickle.

The arrival of the bus was an event, heralding itself by the sound of brakes out in the dark street, the blast of a horn, and the rumbling of a big motor. I was already on my feet, grip in hand, when the uniformed driver threw open the door of the bus and stepped nimbly down onto the pavement. He was a smallish, neat man who was going to no trouble to disguise his good looks. When I presented myself to him, feeling in the pocket where I thought I had put my ticket and not finding it and then feeling in the pocket where I actually had put it and finding it, he looked me up and down with a grin.

"Now I wonder whose daddy this boy is," he said.

While he held out his hand for my ticket, I wasted some of his valuable time in wondering if that question had an answer—though, by now, it has been answered, for years ago I did become somebody's daddy, and in the course of time somebody's granddaddy also.

"Hush up and get on out of here," Miss Angela said from behind me. "He needs to get off at the upper end of Bird's Branch."

He took my ticket, said "Yowzum!" to Miss Angela, and I stepped up into the dim interior of the bus, followed by three or four other passengers. I took a seat by the window just behind the driver and put my grip on the seat beside me. The driver leapt heroically into his seat, closed the door, sealing us within the inward rumble of the motor while he put the gathered tickets into their proper place and readjusted his handsome cap, and then we were off.

Hargrave was a stop on the Greyhound route from Louisville to Cincinnati, but this bus was not one of the Greyhound line. It lacked the insignia of the running hound, which I admired excessively, and it made its humble journey from Hargrave to Louisville by way of the back roads, gathering eventually a pretty full load of shoppers and people whom I believe we had not yet learned to call "commuters." It was a lesser dog than a greyhound, but I had never ridden in such a vehicle before and I was duly impressed by its size and power and by the height of my plush seat, which permitted me to look down upon the tops of mere automobiles. We rolled out of Hargrave and over the bridge into Ellville, there turning away from the valley of the Ohio into the valley of what we, who still belonged more to Port William than to Hargrave, called "our river."

I could look back then at the lights of Hargrave disappearing behind us. Soon even the glow of them was out of sight, and the bus was enclosed in the darkness of the night-bound country-side, broken only by its own headlights and those of a car or two, and here and there by the lighted kitchen windows of the farmhouses. So I remember the nighttimes of my childhood, when the darkness enclosed separately our scattered human lights.

Only now and again we met a car. The cars, like our bus, were going slowly, observing the wartime speed limit. There were limits of all kinds in those days, enough of them to keep even a child reminded that over across the oceans people were fighting and being hurt or killed every hour of every day and night. When I thought of the war I thought of my uncle Virgil, who was in the army. He had not yet been sent overseas. He was safe so far. But as it would turn out he would, as we feared, be sent overseas and into the fighting. He would, as we feared, be killed, though for a long time we knew for sure only that he was "missing."

"Missing," my mother said, "means that we don't know, but we must hope. We must hope and pray." She would say that, smiling, and then look away to hide the tears that I knew were in her eyes. Uncle Virgil was her brother, seven years younger than she was, and I had some idea how much she loved him. I understood her tears better than I understood hope and prayer.

Uncle Virgil's wife was Hannah, who lived now with my Feltner grandparents. Hannah was beautiful and very kind. Sometimes we had long conversations together in which she told me how things had been with her when she was a girl. I was deeply and sweetly in love with her, as only a small boy can be in love with a young woman who is beautiful and kind. I wanted to marry somebody just like her as soon as I would be grown up.

I had picked up a good deal of hearsay about what happens between men and women when they are married, some of it outlandish enough, but I was having trouble applying it to any of the married people I actually knew. In the secrecy of my heart I imagined my own marriage as a sort of official permit to adore some lady as beautiful and kind as Hannah, perhaps in the manner of one of the knights of the Round Table, and to do daring deeds that would cause her to adore me.

While the bus plodded along at thirty or so miles an hour, which was maybe fast enough on that crooked road, my mind, under the influence of my first cup of coffee and four spoonsful of sugar, seemed to be going at the speed of light. I seemed to be thinking of everything at once, my mind darting about in midair like a dragonfly. I was sitting straight up on the edge of the seat, my eyes as wide open as possible, looking past the driver at the lighted road and then into the darkness outside my window and then around at the other passengers, in some danger of twisting my head off. The darkness was growing lighter. I began to see the trees and houses along the road. As we passed through the open bottomlands I could see way off on the far side of the river the hills dark against the brightening sky. We made two or three stops for new passengers who hailed us from the roadside. They stepped aboard, paid their fare, and found seats.

And then I recalled in a flash of panic that the Bird's Branch road had two ends, a lower end and an upper end. I got up, holding to the post at the head of the aisle, and tapped the driver on the shoulder. I said, "I need to get off at the *upper* end of the Bird's Branch road."

The driver nodded a big nod without looking away from the road. He said, "Never fear, Mr. Catlett. I will set you down on the spot."

❧

As good as his word, and to my relief, since I had had time once again to poison my jittering mind with distrust and panic, he let me off right at the designated spot. The bus stopped with a great hiss, the door clapped open, I stepped down and out, and the door clapped shut behind me. The gargle of its idling motor rose into a kind of resolve. The sound of it accelerated and diminished, and then it was gathered into silence. And I was standing in the cold wind at the opening of the Bird's Branch road, the upper end, where my grandfather, Marce Catlett, and his colored hired hand, Dick Watson, were waiting for me.

They had come with the team and wagon, the grain box still on the running gear from the corn harvest, the two old men sitting side by side on the spring seat, Dick handling the mules and my grandfather sitting with his hands at rest on the crook of his cane. The good pair of black mare mules had not expected the bus. It was new to their experience, and it had not met their approval. Though it had passed out of hearing by the time I raised my hand in greeting, the mules were still leaning back into their britchings with their ears pointed anxiously forward, and Dick was saying, "Whoa, Beck! Whoa, Cathern! Whoa, girls!" and Grandpa Catlett, having been as distrustful of the bus nearly as the mules, was saying for the second time, "Ay God, Dick, there he is!"

I waited to approach the wagon until the team had quieted, and then I handed my grip up to Dick, who lifted it over onto the floor behind the seat. And then, reaching down, he helped me to climb up and onto the seat between them.

He turned the wagon around and we headed home. We could no longer hear any noise from the bigger road at all. The only sounds now were the rattling of the breast chains and traces, the footsteps of the mules, and the rumble of the turning wheels. The Bird's Branch road in those days was still just a two-track graveled lane, wide enough in most places for two vehicles to meet and pass. It was snug sitting there between Grandpa and Dick, and I no longer minded the wind. Before long my caffeinated thoughts had eased from the speed of the bus to the perhaps four-mile-an-hour gait of the mules, which seemed to allow the country to come to rest around me. The mules too had relaxed. They were striding along at a brisk walk, their ears, now that they had abandoned themselves to their work, swaying back and forth as they stepped.

My grandfather, who had been watching them with eager attention, said, "Ay Lord, they're good ones, Dick!" And then, without waiting for Dick to reply, he shook his head in solemn agreement with himself.

It was as though a curtain had fallen on a stage and the credulous audience (I, that is to say) was now in a different world from the one I had waked up in only a short time ago. The world I was in now was an older one that had been in existence a long time, though it would last only a few more years. The time was about over when a boy traveling into the Port William community might be met by a team of mules and a wagon. Dick Watson

would die in the fall of 1945 and Grandpa Catlett in the late
winter of 1946. By 1950 or so most of the horse and mule teams
would have departed from the country. The men and women
who had known only the old ways were departing fast. I knew
well at that time that the two worlds existed and that I lived in
both. During the school year I lived mostly in Hargrave, the
county seat at the confluence of the rivers. Hargrave, though it
seemed large to me, was a small town that loved its connections
with the greater world, had always aspired to be bigger, richer,
and grander than it was, and had always apologized to itself for
being only what it was. When school was out, I lived mostly in
the orbit of the tiny village of Port William, which, so long as it
remained at the center of its own attention, was entirely satisfied to be what it was.

That those two worlds were in mortal contention had never
occurred to me. When in a few years one had entirely consumed
the other, so that no place anywhere would ever again be satisfied to be what it was, I was surprised, and I am more surprised
now by the rapidity of the change than I was then. In only a
few years the world of pavement, speed, and universal dissat-
isfaction had extended itself into nearly every place and nearly
every mind, and the old world of the mule team and wagon
was simply gone, leaving behind it a scatter of less and less intel-
ligible relics.

❧

But on that morning in 1943 I had no premonition of such an
ending. In my innocence, I thought only that the world the

mules were drawing us into was a truer world than the world of Hargrave, and I liked it better. It was a world placed unforgettably within the weather, in the unqualified daylight and darkness. I thought it had always been and would always be pretty much as it was.

And on that morning of my journey I was happy to be sitting scrunched on the wagon seat between the two old men, one black and one white, both of whom I loved. Dick I loved for his never-failing kindness to me, his ready companionship, his lore of horses and mules and fox hounds. My love for Grandpa was more complicated, varyingly mixed with awe and sometimes with fear, for he was a monument and a force.

Though bent a little at the hips from age and wear, he was tall and lean, straight-backed even then. He sat upright on the wagon seat as a man would sit who was mounted assuredly on a good horse, as he had been on many days of his life and as he would be still for another year or two. He carried a heavy stockman's cane that he sometimes leaned on but when walking seldom touched to the ground; at times he did without it altogether. He had been at one time a horse trainer; for a longer time he had been a trader in livestock, riding to court days in the nearby county seats to buy weanling calves or mules and in all weather driving them home; and always and above all he had been a farmer. He was born during the Civil War in the place where he lived all his life, and where he would die. For much of his life times had been hard, and he had struggled just to hold onto the farm. At the time when my father came home with his law degree and by his earnings reinforced the family's hold on the place, it had been in danger of being sold for taxes.

And so my brother Henry and I, born just soon enough to know him a little, were not merely the descendants of his blood; as he saw us, we belonged to a line of succession that had maintained itself in that place by struggle, and we therefore had to be prepared to continue the struggle. His love for us therefore was rarely indulgent, and it could be extremely demanding, burdened as it was by a fearful tenderness and an expectation that was and would be difficult to bear.

He would, for instance, halt in front of us the team he was working and demand to know which mule was in the lead, which was the best in conformation, and if they were hitched right. And how many inches made a hand? And did we know gee from haw?

If our answers were good, he would snort with approval. "Ay God, that's right!"

If we were wrong, he would revert to his opinion that we were still unfit to be weaned. "You ought to be at the house sucking your mammy!" And then, to the team, *"Come up!"*

I have in mind a vision of him that must come from near the end of his working life. He is bareheaded, wearing a pair of bib overalls, a blue shirt, a pair of leather leggings. It is a bright, windy day. He is walking rapidly, leading a young mule from the barn to the pasture behind the barn. His shirt is billowing in the wind. The mule, excited by the wind's commotion and by the imminence of freedom, is dancing sideways on the lead rein. My grandfather, paying the mule no mind whatever, is holding the rein in his right hand but leaning leftward away from the mule. With his left hand he is pinching shut first one nostril and then the other, blowing his nose freely into the air.

And so they disappear around the corner of the barn, the mule capering to the right, snot flying to the left, and that blue shirt fluttering in the wind.

I loved him first of all, I think, in a sort of homage that I did not consciously give and he did not consciously require. Something in his aspect and his bearing called love from me, as if love were not so much a common bond as a common condition of both our lives. I loved him also because I knew that he loved me, and because, when he was pleased with me, he could be intently gentle, as my father could be also.

I love him now more than I did then, for now, sixty-some years later, I understand that his life had been lived in devotion to our place here and its creatures, as my own life, in its way, also has been lived. And I know now how to value his passion for good crops, good animals, and good work, and how to appreciate his grief when he failed to live up to his passion. For he had known failure, as he would acknowledge bluntly, as he acknowledged everything else. He had too rarely been free of the stress of debt, and therefore of haste and overwork. He had been compelled by the urgencies of debt to put his land too much at risk, and he and it had paid the inevitable costs. His life, his very flesh, had been shaped by weather, work, and the struggle to keep what he had and what he loved.

❦

The town of Port William stands less than a mile from the river on an upland deeply grooved by branching valleys and hollows. The human geography of the countryside around it is inscribed by roads winding out along open ridges that give way at their edges to wooded bluffs, and by roads winding through the valleys of the larger streams.

The road we were following that morning lies, widened and paved now, along one of the ridges, bending this way and that, rising and falling, according to various compromises between topography and property lines and its own inclination toward the level and the straight. In the swags the road dipped down almost to touch the thickets at the upper ends of the wooded hollows. On the rises of the ground we could see ahead of us, at varying angles and ever closer, the house and barns and other outbuildings of what we still call "the home place." It is where my brother Henry now lives.

From the next-to-last rise we could see also the bare woods below the house, and the small house at the woods' corner where Dick lived. We could see the smoke rising from the chimneys of the two houses, and smoke also from the corner of the tobacco barn where Jess and Rufus Brightleaf and whoever was helping them were at work in the stripping room, preparing the crop for market. We could see Rufus's run-down old car parked in the lot in front of the feed barn. These signs gave the place a look of coherence and calm, all its purposes clear and intact. Before long the kitchens would begin to fill with the smells of dinner cooking. The sense of the place came to me, the whole of it. The place, the season, the weather, the work going on—how I loved it!

The weather too felt relatively calm in the draws, but on the rises, where the long wind drove unobstructed across the distances, we felt the cold, for the night's frost still lay on the fields.

It was cloudy. The days since Christmas had been, not bitterly cold, but merely windy and raw with spats of drizzle, freezing rain, or snow, just enough to keep the bare ground muddy when it thawed. Now a few snowflakes were again in the air, drifting down laggardly in the sheltered places but on the high ground flying straight across so that they did not seem to fall.

When we had driven up past the woods and the pasture above it and the mailbox, and turned finally through the front gate and started up the drive toward the house, I had begun to look forward to Grandma's kitchen and the warmth of the stove and maybe a leftover biscuit or batter cake to tide me over until dinnertime.

Turning into that gate was not, for me, merely the entrance into a place. I was also entering my sense, almost my memory, of my father's childhood; of his pet coon; of his pony; of his friend, the white hired hand, John Penley, who played the banjo and took him hunting; of his friend, the black hired hand, Saul Demint, who could play his own head like a musical instrument; of the day my father's fingers were caught by the falling lid of the flour bin and Grandma walked the yard with him while he suffered and cried; of the family's sometime economic despair; of his going away to school. And I had at least one memory, vividly colored in my imagination, of Grandpa's childhood: the night the old brick house where he was born caught fire. He was six years old. He had saved his money and bought a saddle, which he kept under his bed, and he saved his saddle from the fire. Before that I had a memory, dark and indistinct, only a feeling really, of the Civil War and some soldiers coming in the night to take away my great-grandfather, in an attempt to make a soldier of him, and his rescue by my great-grandmother—all this while Grandpa was "just a little bit of a baby laying up yonder in the bed."

Dick stopped the team as we drew even with the back of the house, gave me a hand to get down, and handed me my grip.

I gave him a wave and said, "Thank you, Dick."

He grinned at me, his teeth tobacco-stained under his mustache, raised his hand, and said, "You're welcome, buddy."

❦

Henry and I called Dick Watson "Dick" in defiance of good manners and the instructions of my white elders who wanted us to call him "Uncle Dick," and who finally, unprevailing, gave up. Dick called me, as he called my brother, "buddy." However consciously it was done, and at least on Henry's and my part it was not done very consciously, our so naming one another put our friendship at an angle to the custom of the time and place in which Dick and my grandfather were to each other "Dick" and "Boss." As far as I was concerned, I called Dick "Dick" and he called me "buddy" because we were buddies and that was that. My love for him, which the years have not diminished, was not, in my own mind, affected at all by considerations of race. To me, he was merely himself. And perhaps, in his affection for me, I was merely myself: a young boy, a listener, not too much trouble, sometimes useful, good sometimes for company, and manifestly devoted to him. Our friendship was a small reality within a larger reality that granted little importance to it.

Whereas my grandfather's life had been shaped by the effort

to keep what he had, Dick's had been shaped by the effort implied in not-having. Dick owned nothing but a few clothes, a few sticks of furniture, a few chickens varying in number according to the success of the foxes and the hawks, and a cheap insurance policy that provided him in the end a decent burial but not a permanent marker for his grave. Never in his life had he owned more than that.

Much earlier in his life Dick had been married to a woman named Etta, of whom he would occasionally speak with affection and sorrow. They had no children. Now he lived with Aunt Sarah Jane, also childless, and they had each other for support in their declining years. I spent a lot of time with them, separately and together, and I never heard them utter an unpleasant word about each other or to each other.

Dick would be felled by a stroke one morning as he stepped out the door to go to work, and he would die that evening before dark. Jess and Rufus Brightleaf, who were already at the barn, helped Aunt Sarah Jane to get him out of the open doorway where he had been lying in the cold and into bed. As soon as she heard, my grandmother went to give what help she could, which was not much. She told me that when she went into the room Dick looked at her, in his terrible stillness, as though he had something he longed to say, but he could not speak. And in all the years since, that look, which I did not see, has stayed in my memory. He never moved or spoke again. After his burial in the "colored graveyard" at Port William, his grave had for a while a metal marker that finally rusted away or was lost, and then a few people remembered, until they died, where his grave was, and now nobody knows.

When the sunlight came through clouds in visible shafts, he would say, "Sun's drawing water."

When it was dry and the crescent moon lay on her back, he would say, "Moon's holding water in her lap."

Of a fine saddle mare he had known once he would say, "You be standing half a mile off, you'd hear her hit the pike: racka-tacka racka-tacka racka-tacka!"

❧

Time and history being as they are, it is not possible now to think of that long gone aging couple and their household down at the corner of the woods without thinking also of the history of racism. But the history of racism, for anybody involved in it, is a difficulty, for it is a history that exists only as it has been interfused with the life and work of particular times and places and people. Moreover, it is a history with two sides, involving nobody who has experienced both. And now, when the two races are more divided than ever, this history has acquired a conventional oversimplification, implying that what we came to call "segregation" was a highly generalized circumstance in which the two races disliked or hated each other, and which assured the happiness of one race and the misery of the other. And so perhaps I offend current political etiquette, as I offend the racism to which it is opposed, by saying that, in and in spite of the old racial arrangement into which we both were born, I loved Dick Watson, and he treated me with affection and with perfect and unfailing kindness.

In and in spite of that old arrangement with all its implied costs and demands, Dick Watson was a man of consummate dignity. I heard him, one time, ventriloquize rather bitterly a dialogue between "Sambo" and "Massa." I remember this, I think, mainly because of my puzzlement. I didn't know the immediate cause, and I was too little adept in the history of racism to know clearly what he was talking about. I associated the name "Sambo" only with "little black Sambo," whom I regarded as a sort of hero. And as I had not heard the word "Massa" before—the related term that I knew was "Old Marster," by which Grandpa and others of his kind referred to God—I could gather only the vaguest sense of what it meant. But there was no mistaking Dick's tone or Aunt Sarah Jane's wish to hush him, and so I was properly disturbed. I am sure that he must have had other moments of bitterness, but I did not know him as a bitter man. I knew him as a man who had achieved an authentic gentleness.

Owning little, living day to day from his small daily wage, such provender as the farm by agreement furnished, and what he and Aunt Sarah Jane grew or found for themselves, he lived a life that was in some ways less dragged upon by past and future than my grandfather's. He did not live upon accumulations. It seems to me that he was capable, often enough, of life as contemporary as the daily sunlight. Both he and Aunt Sarah Jane loved questing at large in the woods and fields, she for greens and herbs and mushrooms, he for a fox or to see what he could see. Following them about on these travels, I learned to see our country without the stress of requirement or judgment or worry, with only the expectation that at any moment it might reveal something of interest. And so I include them in the ancestry of my mind. My grandfather could not have taught me to see the country as they saw it, for his own history in it pressed too heavily upon him, though I learned also to see it in his way, and his way also has stayed with me and is dear and necessary.

Dick Watson's life would be as unimaginable to most people, black or white, in the present world, as would my grandfather's. As unimaginable and, I am saddened to say, as little honored. Different as they were, they were in significant ways alike. They both belonged entirely to the older world, the world of the team and wagon. They both were born farmers, utterly reconciled to the demands of weather and work. Neither of them expected life to be easy or to get easier, or thought it was supposed to get easier. Both lived and died in a society that depreciated their work, took it for granted, and increasingly held them and others like them in contempt for doing it.

As it would happen, I grew up with a prejudice in favor of what I learned from the two of them. Like my grandfather Catlett, I needed land to hold on to, even if only just a little farm, marginal and rough, here in our home country. And I have needed to do the work that such a place requires. I have held to the land and kept at the work, and the work has kept me reminded of those two old men whose ways I learned when I was a boy. I knew Grandpa only when he was old; I recognize him in myself now that I am old. And when I bend to my work now and feel the protest in my back and hips, I think, "Dick!"

II

Now as, looking back, I see myself standing with my grip in my hand, watching the wagon pull away toward the lot gate and the barns and sheds beyond, the little fluster of snow having sped away over the horizon, I feel again the wind's suddenly surrounding chill, and I know that I once huddled between Dick and Grandpa in the joy of trust and warmth.

The unobstructed wind bit my face and fingers, rattling everything loose, and I ran, wagging the grip, around the back of the house, up the two steps into the screened back porch, letting the door bang behind me, and then through the kitchen door into the dimmer indoor light. I set down my grip and said, "Whoo! It's windy out!"

My grandmother turned from the stove and hurried over to hug me.

"Oh lord, child, you're frozen to death!" she said, feeling the cold in my clothes.

Suddenly hurrying, she snatched off my gloves and chafed my hands between both of hers. She flung down one of my

hands and with the other led me over close to the stove. She
shoved two new sticks of wood into the firebox and opened the
draft, whereupon the fire fairly bellowed with exuberance, and
I caught a fragrant whiff of the fresh locust wood starting to
burn. She dragged a chair out from the table, made me sit down,
took off my toboggan, attempted to make my hair lie down,
and then began unbuttoning my mackinaw, interfering with
my efforts to do the same. Her manner was utterly proprietary,
as if I were perhaps a dog or a doll. It was a performance that
somewhat embarrassed me, even when none of my friends was
around to see it, though now, from a distance of so many years,
I watch with amusement, and also with gratitude.

"Take those overshoes off," she said, "so your feet can get
warm."

When I was too slow in taking them off she yanked them off
herself and put them under the stove.

"Are you hungry?" she asked and, without giving me time to
answer, thrust a cold biscuit into each of my hands.

And then, as I knew she was going to do, she swooped upon
me again and felt of my arms and legs to see if I was getting
warm, discovering in the process that I was still the skinny boy
I had always been.

"You don't have enough fat on you for a frying-size chicken,"
she said. "You'd have to stand twice in the same place to make
a shadow."

But then, satisfied at last that I was getting warm, and that
in spite of my skinniness I was all right and likely to survive,
Grandma fitted herself back into her morning's work. She sat
down and resumed peeling potatoes for dinner. She picked up

the potatoes one at a time from an old wash pan on a chair facing hers, peeling them rapidly, letting the peelings drop all in one piece onto a newspaper spread open in her lap, and placed the peeled potatoes in a stewpot of water on the table beside her. While she worked I was content to sit in the warmth and watch, pleased that just the two of us were there.

I loved that old kitchen with its rude furnishings, and I love the memory of it. Just inside the door I had come in there was a washstand with a water bucket and dipper, a wash pan, and a soap dish. The towel hanging above it from a nail in the door facing was half a flour sack, hemmed up, with a worked buttonhole in each end so that when one end got dirty the clean end could then be used. There was a large iron cooking stove, a cabinet with shelves, a large table bearing many coats of paint and a green-and-white-checkered oilcloth, and eight matching chairs, also deeply encrusted with paint. Four of the chairs were at the table, the others placed conveniently elsewhere. There were two large bins, one for flour, one for stove wood. They were painted like the table and chairs, and a boy could slide down their slanting tops. From a nail in the blistered wainscoting behind the stove hung a turkey wing broom that was used to sweep up ashes and such. Close by would be a gallon paint bucket of coal oil with corncobs soaking in it, to make quick work of starting a fire in the morning. The linoleum carpet was footworn and wet-mopped until it was black and tattery at the edges.

My father, who was anxious that Grandma should have help with her housework now that she was old, was always hiring somebody, some woman, white or black, to come and live in the room over the kitchen and help Grandma, but those women never lasted long. Grandma had her inviolable ways and opinions, and she could not keep herself at peace for very long with anybody. Her antipathies, like her affections, readily mounted to flood stage and flowed with a strong current. But she was full of memories and stories too, that went back to the Civil War and before. I loved to be with her when she was at peace and talkative, and I loved to watch her cook.

Rural electrification was on its way, I suppose, for it would soon arrive, but it had not arrived yet. On the back porch there was a large icebox that, when ice was available, preserved leftovers and cooled the milk in the summer. That and the battery-powered radio and the telephone were the only modern devices in the house. Its old economy of the farm household was still intact. The supply lines ran to the kitchen from the henhouse and garden, cellar and smokehouse, cropland and pasture. On the kitchen table were two quart jars of green beans, a quart jar of applesauce, and a pint jar of what I knew to be the wild black raspberries that abounded in the thickets and woods edges of that time. I thought, "Pie!"

"Are you going to make a pie?" I asked.

"Hmh!" she said. "Maybe. Would you like to have a pie?"

And I said, with my best manners, "Yes, mam."

She was soon done with the potatoes. She shut the draft on the stove, taming the fire, changed the water on the potatoes, clapped a lid onto the pot, and set it on the stove to boil. She got out another pot, emptied the beans into it, added salt, some pepper, and a fine piece of fat pork. She was talking at large, commenting on her work, telling what she had learned from relatives' letters and Christmas cards and from listening in on the party line. I was up and following her around by then, to make sure I got the benefit of everything.

She washed her hands at the washstand by the back door and dried them. I followed her into the cool pantry and watched as she measured out flour and lard and the other ingredients and began making the dough for a pie crust. She rolled out the dough to the right thickness, pressed it into a pie pan, and, holding the pan on the fingertips of her left hand, passed a knife around its edge to carve off the surplus dough.

As it would happen, the two of us would be standing in the same place in the same way on a late afternoon in the coming July, she making, I believe, a pie and I watching, after we had been told that my uncle Andrew, my father's older brother, her firstborn son, had been shot and before we learned that he was dead. And now in my mind this earlier memory seems invested somehow with foreknowledge of the later one. While Dorie Catlett was making her grandson a pie on that day near the end of 1943, granting him the pleasure of watching her make it and then of eating it, they were coming to grief, as she had come before but he had not.

As she went about her preparations for dinner, she was commenting to herself, with grunts of determination or approval, on her progress. I knew even then that it was a wonder to see her at her work, and I know it more completely now. Her kitchen would be counted a poor thing by modern standards. There was of course no electrical equipment at all. The cooking utensils, excepting the invincible iron skillet and griddle, were chipped or dented or patched. The kitchen knives were worn lean with sharpening. Everything was signed with the wear of a lifetime or more. She was a fine cook. She did not do much in the way of exact measurement. She seasoned to taste. She mixed by experience and to the right consistency. The dough for a pie crust or biscuits, for instance, had to be neither too flabby nor too stiff; it was right when it felt right. She did not own a cookbook or a written recipe.

Meanwhile, she had prepared the raspberries, adding flour and sugar to the juice and heating it in a saucepan. Now she poured berries and juice into the dough-lined pan. She balled up the surplus dough, worked it briskly with her hands on the broken marble dresser top that she used for such work, sprinkled flour over it, rolled it flat, and then she sliced it rapidly into strips, which she laid in a beautiful lattice over the filling. As a final touch she sprinkled over the top a thin layer of sugar that in the heat of the oven would turn crisp and brown. And then she slid the pie into the oven.

She was being extravagant with the sugar for my sake, as I was more or less aware, and as I took for granted. But knowledge grows with age, and gratitude grows with knowledge. Now I am as grateful to her as I should have been then, and I am troubled with love for her, knowing how she was wrung all her life between her cherished resentments and her fierce affections. A peculiar sorrow hovered about her, and not only for the inevitable losses and griefs of her years; it came also from her settled conviction of the tendency of things to be unsatisfactory, to fail to live up to expectation, to fall short. She was haunted, I think, by the suspicion of a comedown always lurking behind the best appearances. I wonder now if she had ever read *Paradise Lost*. That poem, with its cosmos of Heaven and Hell and Paradise

and the Fallen World, was a presence felt by most of her genera-
tion, if only by way of preachers who had read it. Whether or
not she had read it for herself, the lostness of Paradise was the
prime fact of her world, and she felt it keenly.

Once the pie was out of the way, she went ahead and made
biscuit dough, flattened it with her rolling pin, cut out the biscuits, and laid them into the pans ready for the oven when the
time would come.

She had cooked breakfast, strained the morning milk, made
the beds, set the house to rights, washed the breakfast dishes,
and cleaned up the kitchen before I got there. Now she let me
help her, and we carried the crocks of morning milk from the
back porch down into the cellar, and brought the crocks of last
night's milk up from the cellar to the kitchen for skimming.

❦

I enjoyed watching her skim the milk and so I stayed until she
had passed the skimmer over the crocks, with a lovely discrimi-
nation gathering the thick yellow cream off the white milk, and
then I said, "Well, I'm going to the barn."

"Oh," she said, "*don't* go back into the cold. Stay here with
Grandma where it's warm."

"It'll be warm in the stripping room," I said. "That's where
I'm going."

She laughed her laugh of resignation. "Well, if you're bound
to go, go," she said. "Go to the mailbox before you come back
and bring the mail."

"I will," I said. "I will I will I will."

I put on my overshoes, mackinaw, toboggan, and gloves, and went out. It was a little past the middle of the morning, but it was still cold, close to freezing, and the wind was still blowing. To face the weather again after the warm kitchen required a moment of courage, but I was soon glad to be out in the big daylight, looking around. I went into the barn lot and past the woodpile, and Grandma's dog, old Ring, came out to meet me from the feed barn where he had been holed up. I spoke to him and gave him a pat or two and went on into the barn to see what was going on there. Except for Beck and Catherine, all the stock had been turned out. The place felt deserted. In the quiet I could hear the two mules eating hay from their mangers. They were tied in their stalls, unbridled but still wearing their harness in case they would be needed.

From the feed barn, I went through the two gates of the loading chute lot into the small field in front of the tobacco barn. The two milk cows and a Hereford bull were in that field, and where they had stood in front of the barn to be out of the wind the ground was deeply tracked. A little snow had collected in the bottom of the tracks. The sliding doors of the barn were shut, but a broken board in one of them made a crack just wide enough for me to squeeze through. As soon as I was inside and out of the wind, I could hear voices I knew coming from the stripping room.

Along one side of the driveway there was a large "bulk" of unstripped tobacco, walled around with standing bundles of sorghum and covered with old rugs to keep the tobacco moist and handleable. On the other side next to the stripping room, which occupied one of the front corners of the barn, was the tobacco that had been stripped, graded, tied in "hands," pressed, and laid into a second "bulk," this one as carefully composed as a made bed. In the driveway itself was a hay wagon on which they were piling the stripped stalks to be hauled out and scattered.

The voices in the stripping room sound settled and quiet. I let myself stand and listen a minute to the voices and to the wind shoving and shuddering along the eaves of the barn. As I expected, the stripping room door was fastened on the inside. I pounded on it four times with my fist. The voices stopped and there were footsteps. The door opened, and there was Rufus Brightleaf beaming largely down at me with his toothless grin.

"*Yaaah!*" he said. "*Come* in here, fart blossom." And I stepped into the warmth. He grinned at me until I grinned back, and then he said, "Ha-*hahhh!*" and gave me a big handshake. In his large, hard hand my own felt small and soft.

Jess Brightleaf said, "Hello, Andy," and Dick Watson said, "Howdy, buddy." The one known as Old Man Hawk neither turned to look at me nor spoke. Rufus fastened the door and went back to work.

They were standing at the bench under the row of north windows in an order I knew, first Rufus then Jess then Dick then Old Man Hawk, each man stripping the leaves that belonged to his grade and passing the stalks on to the next man, from Rufus finally to Old Man Hawk, who was stripping the least valuable grade known as "tips" and carrying the stripped stalks out to the wagon. Above each man's section of the bench was hung a strip of pork fat on which from time to time he greased his hands to relieve the stickiness of the tobacco gum.

The Brightleafs were Grandpa's tenants, growing his tobacco crop on the shares. They had come at the beginning of a rare time of good farm prices, and before it ended Jess Brightleaf and his family would save enough money to buy a farm of their own. The departure of the Brightleafs would be another of the changes that brought to an end what had seemed the stable old world of my childhood.

Jess Brightleaf was the master workman of that place and time. He held the honored title of "tobacco man," and he was as meticulous in his work, as watchful of the work of the others, as difficult to please, as if he were practicing a fine art, which in fact he was.

Rufus, Jess's brother, was a man perhaps equally capable but less mindful, less caring, for Rufus was a man prone, during any letup of work, to drink and stray. His wife, Miss Ida, whom he called "the Madam," had been called upon for more in the way of patience than was good for her. He had a gift for amusing himself, and in the process amusing others, with an obscene repertory of tales, rhymes, and songs most certainly unfit for the ears of the Madam. To hear him you would have thought he had not a care in the world, but I knew that he did have. I knew that he and Miss Ida had had two daughters and a son, and that the son was dead. He had been killed by a falling tree when they were cutting sawlogs. Rufus had told me this (I must have asked him where was his son) when we were alone together the summer before, and he had not looked or sounded like himself when he told it. "Poor fellow," he said. "Broke all to hell, and nothing we could do." And perhaps it was because of that boy of his, dead, that Rufus had at times played with me as if he had been another child. I admired Jess and was in awe of him, but I loved Rufus.

Dick Watson was as I have said: cheerful and gentle and steady at his work. He would come to the stripping room after finishing his morning chores at the barn and at Grandpa's house and at his own, and then he would leave early enough to finish his evening chores mostly before dark.

Old Man Hawk worked on with nothing to say. He had a reputation for various acts of dishonesty and violence, a dangerous man, and he was the father of several young men with reputations as terrible as his own. He would work, he was available, and so, in that time of scarce help, he was there. Jess and Mrs. Brightleaf would house and feed and pay him until the work was done, and they would do it with a good-humored deference to necessity. It was his pride, when working, to acknowledge the existence of nothing but work. And yet it was clear to me that he passed his harsh judgment, his utter contempt in fact, upon other people by paying them no mind at all, as if a known chicken thief might regard the world from an exalted standpoint of indifference. His last name, officially, was Hackman, but, since Port William did not pronounce names it had not heard before, from the time of his appearance there from no known origin, he had been called "Hawkman"—"Hawk" to his face and, in his latter years, to his back, "Old Man Hawk."

I was sorry to see him there, for I was afraid of him. One day Dick Watson had confided to me: "Buddy, don't never let him hear you say 'Hawk got a chicken and gone to the stack.' He'll kill you." Because it was Dick who told me this, I believed it. And every time I had to be in his presence, the feeling would come over me that I was about to say "Hawk got a chicken and gone to the stack." I feared him because of that, and also because of the look of him. In contrast to Jess's face, which, at work, was contemplative, and Rufus's, which was florid and as variable as a baby's, and Dick's, which was gentle and patient, Old Man Hawk's was blank and hard and somehow pinched, as if it had been frostbitten or burnt.

Grandpa was sitting close to the stove on an upturned five-gallon bucket. He was too old to be much good for work anymore, but he needed to stay close to it. He turned a bucket up for me beside him. "Here, baby. Sit down and keep out of the way."

I sat down and let myself come to rest in the warmth and in the fragrance of the tobacco. Dick would have built the fire first thing that morning on his way up to the barn to feed and milk, and the thin-walled room, constructed of odds and ends of old lumber and corrugated roofing, by now was thoroughly warm. The men at the bench were working rapidly, but their talk was leisurely. I leaned back against the wall, making myself comfortable, for I loved their talk.

"Well, Dick," Jess Brightleaf said, "looks like you all met that bus all right. I reckon you got there in plenty of time."

Dick laughed his laugh—"Ho-ho-ho!"—that meant he wasn't going to tell all that he might. "Yessir, Mr. Jessie. We was out at the pike wasn't even day yet."

He would tell me later that Grandpa had been talking about meeting the bus for two or three days. That I would be coming by myself was a matter that he had taken very seriously. That my father would have entrusted me alone to such a contraption as a bus had not met Grandpa's approval. He did not understand internal combustion as a motive force, and he regarded it with a mixture of deference and awe and deep suspicion.

"Ay Lord," Grandpa said, "there was the little thing with his satchel, come all that way by himself." He spoke as if he had witnessed an event of great pathos and wonder, never mind that at my age he would have ridden so far on horseback alone and thought nothing of it.

Jess Brightleaf looked around at us, amused, and said, "Uncle Marce, looks like the boy has fattened up right sharply."

"Aw," Rufus said, "he swells up that way *ever'* winter." He turned around and, grinning, squeezed experimentally my thigh above the knee. "*Ain't* that right, Andy?"

"A many a good biscuit has gone down that boy," Jess said. "He eats so much it makes him poor to carry it."

"Yaaa-*hahaaa*!" Rufus said. "That boy traded legs with a grasshopper and got cheated out of a ass."

"Well," Jess said considerately, "he'll grow. He'll fill out. We'll get him up here with us next summer and work him hard and put some of that fried chicken and a few biscuits into him, you won't know him by fall."

So they greeted me, made much of me, gave me very astutely my credit rating, and so reminded me how much, how much more than they knew, I wished to grow and fill out and do work worthy of my dinner. When all their backs were turned again, I felt for myself the place where Rufus's hard handprint still lay on my thigh, and I had to acknowledge that it was sure enough a rather grasshopperly appendage.

Jess's allusion to the coming summer, which by the last of December would have been already on his mind, started Rufus into an elaborate prophecy of the coming hot weather, and so they were done with me for a while. Rufus said that when the weather got hot, *this* time around, he would have a few bottles of beer soaking in a tub of ice under a shade tree at the edge of the tobacco patch. "And then when we go down one of them long rows and the old sun's cracking down and the sweat's running in our eyes and we're dry as a popcorn fart, we'll rear back in that shade and turn up one of them good old cold ones. *Ain't* that right, Uncle Marce?" He let go his big yell of a laugh, and Grandpa snorted and said, "Ay Lord, Rufus!"

Everybody knew, even I knew, so well that he would do no such thing, that Jess Brightleaf would have tolerated no such thing, that there was no further need for comment.

They worked on in silence a while and then, introducing the subject with a little laugh, Jess told how Rufus, well filled with beer in his younger days, had stretched out to sleep it off in the shade of a big oak tree in a pasture. After a while the shade moved off, and Rufus began to sweat in the hot sun. The cows came up, as cows are apt to do at any curious sight, and, smelling the salt in Rufus's sweat, they ate his shirt off of him while he slept.

The Brightleaf brothers, like many farmers of our region who belonged to that old world that ended with mechanization in the aftermath of the war, were men who talked for pleasure. They talked to keep their minds employed, to entertain themselves, to lighten their weariness, for companionship. No silence could last very long before one of them would need to have something to say. While they talked Grandpa would chime in from time to time with a comment or a word of confirmation or commendation; from time to time their stories would remind him of a story he remembered and he would tell it. He had begun to ponder the days of his youth, as old men do, and the stories he told were of a time nobody else remembered. Dick Watson mostly listened, laughing or nodding or shaking his head. Old Man Hawk paid so little regard that he might as well have been deaf, or not there at all.

They talked about the weather and what it had done and might do. They talked about the quality of this crop, and of last year's, and of the crops of other years. They talked of the tobacco market and prices and of the time, coming soon, when the present crop would be taken to the warehouse and sold.

Rufus said, "When we sell this crop, Uncle Marce, let's me and you go to Louisville and rent one of them penthouses. We'll lay in a good stock of that bottled-in-bond and plenty to eat. We'll get us a couple of old women about eighteen or twenty years old to cook for us and see to our every need." He was half hollering to make sure Grandpa got the full benefit of this vision, another that even I knew would never be realized. "How *'bout* it, old boss?"

Grandpa snorted and laughed. "Ay Lord, Rufus, we'll do that."

And then, after a silence that had stretched somewhat thin, Rufus sang a song about Old Aunt Dinah who was "a good old soul," in which it was revealed that the word "soul" had the misfortune to rhyme with "hole."

Presently they spoke of the man they called "Mr. Roosyvelt"

and of the war. They marveled at the terrible destructions that had been accomplished, at what bombs could do, at how far the big guns were able to shoot. The war frightened them as it did me, and in our fear we all clung to the thought of President Roosevelt, who consoled us, maybe just by the jaunty way he held his cigarette holder in his teeth, and gave us hope. The Brightleafs, like most of the farming people, pronounced the o's in the first syllable of the president's name as they pronounced the o's in "roof," for it was a name they frequently read in the newspaper but seldom heard.

In that stripping room the next winter, I heard Rufus Brightleaf speaking in awe of "rowboat bombs." He meant "robot bombs," the V-2 rockets that were then flying across the English Channel to fall upon London. But I was still perfectly gullible, still able to believe almost anything I was told by a grownup, and from Rufus's talk of "rowboat bombs" that could "fly clean across the water" I derived a vision at once horrible and absurd. In 1943 the V weapons were a horror as yet unrevealed. The war had many horrors still to be revealed.

Thoughts of the war led them to speak of Tom Coulter, Jarrat Coulter's boy, who had been killed in the fighting in Italy. I was a little kin, on my father's side, to Tom Coulter. His name, as they spoke it in that little room within the barn within the wind within the story of the world, seemed to me to enter the day like a bell stroke. They spoke his name perhaps with the awareness that now his name would be spoken less and less until it would be spoken no more, for they were silent again afterwards.

And then Rufus said quietly, "Boys, he'll be a long time gone from here." As he spoke he had again that look on his face that

I had seen before, that did not look like him, and he did not sound like himself. In my brief knowledge, I thought I knew what he meant. And now, in my long knowledge, I know what he meant.

❦

Soon after that we heard a car drive past the house and stop in front of the feed barn. I was afraid for a minute that it was my father. All through this visit of mine, and especially during my stay at the Catlett home place, I was dogged by the thought that my father or my uncle Andrew would show up, as I reckoned they were likely to do. This thought was merely a trouble in my mind then, for I could not have explained it to myself, but of course if one of them had shown up, driving the ten or so miles from Hargrave as they routinely did, then the charm of my solitary bus trip would have been dispelled; my great adventure would have been revealed to be as trivial as in fact it was. If they did *not* show up, as fortunately they did not, then I would take the bus home late on New Year's Day, and my myth of my first journey alone would complete itself and remain intact in my mind from then on.

I need not have worried, for the car was only Jess Brightleaf's, and, hearing it, he took out his watch, looked at it, and said with much satisfaction, "Bean time." He stepped to the door and opened the latch.

And soon Jess's wife, Ruth, came into the room, carrying dinner and the necessary tableware in two large handbaskets. She was followed by their boy, Fred, who was a year older than

I, and Fred was carrying another basket and a large coffeepot. Daylight was precious then, in the shortest days, and Jess was seeing to it that nobody went home for dinner. They were eating where they worked and stopping work only to eat.

Ruth Brightleaf was a stout, hearty woman, capable at any work of farm or household. "Why, it's Andy! Hello, Andy honey!" she said. "Look, Fred! Andy's here!"

Fred and I were friends and glad enough to see each other, but we couldn't rise to whatever her enthusiasm required of us, and so we just said hello.

Fred was the only child I knew of about my own age who had been gravely ill. He had spent weeks in the hospital, had been operated on by surgeons, and had a long scar to show for it. They were afraid for a while that he would die. And so there was this knowledge about Fred that qualified everything else you knew about him: He had been to death's door and had come back. He had come all the way back, for he was a lively boy, always ready for fun, and he had the hearty way of talking and the big laugh that belonged to all the Brightleafs.

A bucket of water for handwashing had been sitting on the drum stove. Mrs. Brightleaf set it on the floor and in its place put the coffeepot and the several vessels of food. The men, meanwhile, were clearing as much of the bench as they would need for a sort of table or sideboard. The smells of food had begun almost to overpower the smell of tobacco. Mrs. Brightleaf was a good cook, "as good as a man ever ate after," as Grandpa said and I well knew, and she loved to feed boys. I longed to stay and eat and talk with Fred, but Grandpa was already going out, praising Mrs. Brightleaf and her cooking as he went, and I followed as I knew I had to do.

"Come back soon as you eat, Andy," Fred said. "I got a BB gun."

"I'll be right back," I said as I followed Grandpa out the door.

I followed Grandpa through the gates up into the barn lot, and old Ring came out of his hole again to see if he could be of any help. So then the three of us walked in a line across the lot and through the third gate into the backyard.

"Grandma told me to go get the mail," I said.

"That's right, baby," Grandpa said. "Go get it."

And so Ring and I went down through the long yard to the mailbox. There was nothing in it but the newspaper, and I knew Grandma would be disappointed, for the arrival of a letter or postcard from one of our far-away relatives was a great event to her, but I anyhow would have the funnies.

I went around the house and in at the kitchen door, pried off my overshoes, handed the paper to Grandma, took off my wraps, and washed my hands.

"Try combing that hair of yours," Grandma said. "Nobody ever saw the like. It's a regular straw stack."

Knowing it would do no good, I took the comb from the shelf where the water bucket sat and passed it several times through my hair.

Grandma watched me, and then she laughed. "You *are* the limit!" Her laugh was affectionate and indulgent, and yet it was a laugh with a history, conveying her perfected assurance that some things were hopeless. "Well, give up," she finally said. "Come and eat."

She had made a splendid dinner, a feast, little affected by wartime stringencies, which, except for the rationing of coffee and sugar, were little felt in such households. It hadn't been long since hog-killing, and so there was not only a platter of fresh sausage but also a bowl of souse soaking in vinegar. There was a bowl of sausage gravy, another of mashed potatoes, another of green beans, another of apple sauce. There was a pan of hot biscuits, to be buttered or gravied, and another in the oven. There was a handsome cake of freshly churned butter, the top marked in squares neatly carved with the edge of the butter paddle. There was a pitcher of buttermilk and one of sweet milk. And finally there was the pie, still warm, the top crust crisp and sugary and brown.

Oh, I ate as one eats who has not eaten for days, as if my legs were hollow, as if I were bigger inside than outside, and Grandma urged me on as if I were her champion in a tournament of eating.

Grandpa began the meal protesting that he was not hungry, but he ate, as Grandma said, "with a coming appetite," and when it came it came in force. Before my time he had ridden horseback the five miles to Smallwood where his friend the atheist doctor Gib Holston had pulled all his teeth, but he "gummed it" as fast as I could chew with teeth, and he had more capacity.

We ate and said little, for all of us were hungry. The food, as I see now but did not then, looked beautiful laid out before us on the table. And never then did I know that it was laid out in such profusion in honor of me. It was offered to me out of the loneliness of Grandma's life, out of her disappointments, her craving for small comforts and pleasures beyond her reach, to which Grandpa was indifferent. When I had washed down the last bite of my second piece of pie with a final swallow of milk, my stomach was as tight as a tick. I am sure I said "That was good." I may even have said "Thank you," for I was ever conscious that I was traveling alone and therefore in need of my manners. But time has taught me greater thanks.

Grandpa, whose mind was on the stripping room, had eaten without even taking off his coat, his cap and cane hanging from the chairback. The instant he laid down his fork he stood, put on his cap, picked up his cane, and started for the door. That put me in a panic, for I too was thinking of the stripping room and of Fred and of Fred's new BB gun.

"I got to go," I said. And as soon as I could get wrapped up again, I too headed to the door.

Grandma said only "Hmh!" by which she signified to herself and to me that I was doing exactly as she had known I would do, which was exactly as Grandpa had done, which was exactly what she had known he would do.

❧

The stripping room was almost mysteriously the same as it had been through the morning. All signs of dinner were gone, and Mrs. Brightleaf was gone. The men standing at the bench had resumed the preoccupation and the rhythm of their work, which continued as if it had not been interrupted by dinner, or by anything else, perhaps for years. Behind them, unnoticed,

Grandpa was dozing on his bucket by the stove and Fred was
sighting his BB gun through the window.

"Look a here," he said as I came in, and he held the gun out
to show me.

"Boy!" I said, for I was longing for a BB gun of my own, and all
the more keenly because I was forbidden to have one. BB guns
were infamous with my mother for shooting boys in the eye.

Fred aimed the gun out the window between Rufus and Dick
and said, "Pow!"

"Don't point that thing at anybody," Jess said. "Didn't I tell
you?"

Fred didn't answer. He raised the barrel toward the ceiling.

"Didn't I?" Jess said.

"Yes," Fred said.

Rufus said: "Santy brought me one of them things when I
was a boy. First thing I did with it was shoot the old man in the
ass while he was bent over tying his shoe. That was when the
bobbling pin flew off the wobbling shaft. He snatched the gun
away from me and I thought he was going to hit me with it. I
thought 'Katy bar the door,' but he just hit it on a tree, which
didn't do anything to it but cock it again, and went on in the
house. I climbed the tree for fear he still might whip me and
looked in through the window, and there the old man was with
his britchies down, showing my mother a black streak where
that BB had sort of scooted."

We all laughed.

Fred sighted the gun up at the ceiling. "You reckon it would
shoot through that tin?"

"Try it and see," I said.

Without looking at us or stopping work, Jess said, "You boys get out of here with that damned gun."

He meant it, and so we went. We went down the hill to the woods. Old Ring, who had been lying in the barn, got up and came along.

Having a gun, we were going hunting, of course. We thought old Ring might tree a squirrel, which he had sometimes done when we were not armed. And he did tree a squirrel as we were going into the woods, and the squirrel took his stand in the very top of a tall hickory. We wasted a good many BBs in shooting at him, but the squirrel understood the effective range of our weapon better than we did, for he did not move and we did not hit him; if we had hit him with a BB at that height, he would have laughed at us.

We were, in truth, not good hunters. We were bloodthirsty enough, for we shot at every living thing we saw, and we had the firepower to have killed at least a bird if we could have got close enough, but we made too much noise, talked too much, played too much, were too distracted. Intending slaughter, we delivered only the poor mercy of our incompetence. And so when we had shot up all of Fred's BBs, it was a sort of relief. The woods, down there under the hill out of the wind, was quiet and inviting. When we had quit hunting, we spent a while just wandering about. We went to our tree that branched low enough to the ground so we could climb it, and we climbed it right to the top where the trunk was limber and we could feel the wind bending it, and we swung it, making it bend farther. We said we were riding the wind.

At the very back of the woods there was an enormous old

white oak that had stood there, as Grandma said a little wist-
fully, "Oh, since the times of old." Near it, the summer before,
Fred and Henry and I had built a sort of tepee by leaning a lot
of old fence rails against a young hickory. The farm had once
been fenced entirely with rock fences and rail fences. But in the
time of my memory they all were gone, replaced with woven
wire, except for a short stretch of rail fence on the other side
of the ridge below the feed barn. The old rails, some of which
had probably been split from chestnut trees before the blight,
had been ricked up beside the woods to be out of the way and
for use mostly as fuel. Our tepee, anyhow, had been a mighty
work, an ample room within the larger enclosure of the woods.
When we covered it with leafy branches it gave a fine feeling of
shelter, an inside neatly divided from the outside. But now, on
that bare wintry day, the sheltery feeling and the charm were
gone. Our tepee was just a bunch of old rails leaning against a
tree. And that disillusionment ended our adventure in the woods
for the day.

We went back up the hill into the barn lot. In those days there
was a long building on one side of the lot that incorporated the
corncrib, the wagon shed, what we still called the buggy shed
though there was no longer a buggy, and the stall where Dick
milked the cows. Over the cowstall was a loft where hay could
have been stored, but it was now only a catchall for useless things
too good to throw away. Disregarded by the grownups, it was
an excellent place to be out of sight and out of mind.

Fred and I went up the ladder on the wall of the building and
into the loft. The main attraction up there was an old trunk filled
with books. The books were a numbered set, all alike, thick and

heavy and filled with big words, charts, graphs, and tables. Neither of us could read those books, and yet they fascinated us. We called them "the New Orleens books" because their covers were of the same light brown as the cane syrup that we knew as "New Orleens molasses," and because "New Orleens" sounded exotic and important. What they were remains a mystery to this day, for long before we ever read even the titles on their spines, they disappeared. But to open that trunk and to take those books out one by one and look into them made us feel like archaeologists unearthing a tomb inscribed in an unknown language.

Fred and I opened the trunk, withdrew the ice-cold volumes, and looked into them, letting the mystery of them come upon us, and then put them back and closed the lid. And then, without the least sense of incongruity, we chanted a poem we had learned from Rufus which seemed to us both extraordinarily funny and deeply mysterious, and which revealed that "truck" was another English word with a misfortunate rhyme.

By then we were cold. Even in the shelter of the little loft, inactivity had let the weather seep into our clothes. We became conscious of our visible breath and of the numbness of our toes and fingers.

"Let's go."

We hurried down the ladder and back to the stripping room, where we took off our gloves and overshoes and got close to the stove.

As soon as we were warm again, Jess sent Fred home across the fields to help his mother with the evening chores. Not long after that, Dick Watson left to do his own chores, and I went with him.

I walked beside him, holding his hand. As we came up to the first gate an airplane came over, and we stopped and watched it.

I said, "Dick, do you reckon an airplane could fly all the way to Heaven?"

"Can't do it, buddy," he said.

"Why?"

"After a ways it gets tough up there. They can't make it."

That was a relief to me. I thought, "Good!"

Dick and I went to the feed barn first. He unharnessed Beck and Catherine, led them out to drink at the well, and gave them the corn that he had let me carry in from the crib. As often as he could, Dick gave me work to do, because I was always begging to help, but also, I think now, to keep me out of his way or out of danger. When not in the company of other boys, I was inclined to be dreamy. I could slide right out of the present world, right out of the *dangers* of the present world, into the world of Robin Hood or the Swiss Family Robinson or King Arthur and his knights. Or, on the contrary, I could be recklessly eager to help. And so I was rather often in danger without knowing it, especially around large animals. My reveries and enthusiasms were accustomed to be intruded upon by voices from the responsible world: "Look out, Andy!" "Wake up, Andy!" "Mind now, baby!" "Get out of the way!" My father once went so far as to hit me on the shoulder with his fist in imitation of a mule's kick: "*That's how it'll feel, only harder!*"

Dick was never so emphatic, but he too was obliged again and again to remind me where I was: "Wait now, buddy!" "Watch out, buddy!" "Buddy, get back!" But he was more patient than my father and grandfather, and I tried hard to be alert when I was with him.

Dick, as I have just said again, was kind to me. But of course my saying this raises the question of what to make of a servant's kindness. There obviously can be no doubt that, if there had been an occasion for such an expectation, my elders would have expected Dick to be kind to me. But there are qualities and degrees of kindness, and a boy is as good a judge of them as anybody. I don't think Dick was kind in response to expectation. He was kind because it was in his character to be so, just as it was in my character to love him for it. We were living in the history of "race relations," to be sure, but, like everybody else, we were living as ourselves in it.

And so when Dick led Beck out of her stall and I was standing too close, he said, "Stand back, buddy," because, like any adult, he did not want to be responsible for getting me hurt, but also he did not want me to get hurt.

I knew both what he meant and how he meant it, and I stood back.

I should have been so tractable in school—but, though I did not yet know it, that barn *was* a school.

We stabled the two other mules and Grandpa's saddle mare and Henry's and my pony that had been out on pasture for the day, and I brought corn for them. We drove Grandpa's coming-yearling steers into the pen in the back of the barn and fastened them up for the night. We climbed up into the loft, and Dick forked down hay for the mules and the mare and the pony and the steers. When we went out at last and drew the sliding doors shut behind us, the barn work was done until morning. The barn then seemed quieted and complete in itself, the animals sheltered for the night. We could still hear them eating after we closed the doors. We went to the cowstall, put in hay and corn for the cows, and while I brought the milk bucket from the house Dick chained them in their places. We got our milking stools, and I sat on mine and watched while Dick sat on his and milked the cows.

I would have carried the milk to the house, but Dick said, "Next year maybe," and so I walked with him and held his hand while he carried the bucket. He set the bucket inside the door of the kitchen where Grandma had the milk crocks and the strainer ready.

And then we went to the woodpile where for a little time again I could really help — or at least where Dick's charity allowed me to believe I was really helping. He brought the crosscut saw from its place under the eave of the wagon shed. And then, he lifting the heavy end and I the light, we laid a long locust pole on the sawbuck. Dick laid the saw across the pole. We each took a handle and began sawing the pole into stove-lengths.

Dick said, "Don't ride the saw, buddy. Don't push, just pull. All right."

When we had sawed enough, Dick picked up his axe and split the thicker lengths at the chopping block. By then the Brightleafs and Old Man Hawk had gone home, and it was getting dark. We gathered armloads of wood as big as we could manage and carried them to the kitchen where we dumped them into the woodbox beside the stove.

I wanted to go down and help Dick at his own woodpile, but Grandma said no to that, and so for me the day was over. Night had come. Grandma had a lighted lamp on the kitchen table.

I took off my wraps and washed my hands and face.

"Go in the living room where your grandpa is and get warm," Grandma said. "We'll have some supper before long."

I went through the cold hall to the living room. Grandpa was sitting in his rocking chair on the dark side of the stove. He didn't say anything. I went around to the other side to Grandma's chair by her stand table where her best lamp was lighted. My grip was on the floor by the table legs. I opened it and got out *The Boy's King Arthur* and sat down.

Seeing me open the book on my lap, Grandpa said, "Ay God, that's right, baby. Go to your book. That's the thing."

I am perfectly sure, now, that he would not have seen a nickel's worth of good in King Arthur and his knights, if he had known of their existence. But he seemed to me then to have extended a great deal of credit to reading about them, and I merely assumed he was right.

He returned to what he called "studying." He sat looking down at his lap, his left hand idle on the chair arm, his right scratching his head, his white hair gleaming in the lamplight. I knew that when he was studying he was thinking, but I did not know what about. Now I have aged into knowledge of what he thought about.

He thought of his strength and endurance when he was

young, his merriment and joy, and how his life's burdens had then grown upon him. He thought of that arc of country that centered upon Port William as he first had known it in the years just after the Civil War, and as it had changed, and as it had become; and how all that time, which would have seemed almost forever to him when he was a boy, now seemed hardly any time at all. He thought of the people he remembered, now dead, and of those who had come and gone before his knowledge, and of those who would come after, and of his own place in that long procession. Looking at me, he must have remembered that his own grandfather had been the first of our name to come into this place, in a time that had seemed ancient to him once, that he now knew to have been almost recent, and that the time from his grandfather to his grandson had been short. He thought of the living and of how they would appear to the dead, until the dead lived again in his thoughts, and the presently living appeared as ghosts of a future yet to come. He thought of the history of his hands. He laid them in his lap and studied them, and he saw that they were hard-used and now almost useless. This was a study he could not have remembered beginning, and surely he knew that it could not be finished, by him or by anybody.

As he studied his memories and thoughts, I studied him, so that I have not forgotten him. And then I opened my book and studied it. I looked at the print, but my mind, like a dull blade, glanced off. It would not bite in, for the English of those pages was old-fashioned; it was strange to everything I knew. When my mother had started reading it to me on Christmas night and the nights following, I had understood it and been charmed by it, but hearing received it more readily than sight, and she had given me the explanations I needed. And so when I opened the book, unable as I felt to read it for myself, I let into the quiet of the room the memory of my mother's voice reading, which was a comfort to me then as it is now. Besides, the book contained full-page illustrations in which the knights wore armor made of metal as brilliant almost as sunlight and the horses were as fierce and beautiful as dream horses come alive. These were to me then almost endlessly worthy of study. And from the opened pages rose then as now, for I still have the book, the sound of my mother's voice reading quietly and yet urgently, as if anticipating all that was to follow: "It befell in the days of the noble Utherpendragon, when he was King of England, that there was born to him a son who in after time was King Arthur." This might have made me homesick, except for the sound of Grandma's footsteps in the hall and the hall door opening.

"Supper's ready, Marce. Come on, Andy."

We ate our supper in the lamplight that glowed over the table and left much of the kitchen shadowy and dim. Grandma had warmed the beans and potatoes from dinner, but instead of sausage, we had slices of her Christmas ham and turkey, and instead of biscuits she had corn battercakes that she kept putting on our plates hot from the griddle and that we also ate with sorghum molasses for dessert.

I stayed after supper to dry the dishes just to be in the kitchen with her, and then we went into the living room, she carrying the lighted lamp, which she set on the mantelpiece above

Grandpa's chair, where again he sat quietly studying his thoughts and scratching his head. She went to her own chair, took her sewing basket and darning onto her lap, and began to thread a needle, which was more of a job now, she said, than it used to be.

At home at night, when we didn't have homework to do, we played the radio, but that had not yet become a habit of this house. The radio sat on the stand table by the front window, its batteries on the floor beneath, waiting to be turned on when there was something especially good to hear: *Renfro Valley* on Saturday night, maybe, or *Wings over Jordan* on Sunday morning. Batteries cost money and they were not to be wasted. Grandma would have turned it on for me if I had asked, but I didn't ask, for there was no shortage of things to do.

I went to the closet—"press" was her term for it—behind Grandma's chair and took out her button box. Every house I visited as a child had a button box. It has disappeared now from every house I know, but then it was a necessary part of household economy. No worn-out garment then was simply thrown away. When it was worn past wearing and patching, all its buttons were snipped off and put into the button box. And then when something old needed a new button, or when something newly made needed a set of buttons, the button box provided. Grandma's was an old shoe box better than half full of buttons of all sorts. It was a pleasure just to run your fingers through, like running your fingers through a bucket of shelled corn. My old game with it was to paw through it in search of matching sets of buttons, especially the intensely colored glass buttons that had come off dresses. I sat on the floor by Grandma's chair with the box in my lap and fished out a set of shapely black buttons and lined them up on the linoleum beside me.

And then it came to me that I was no longer interested in button boxes. Maybe it was because I was now traveling away from home by bus, by myself, but I knew suddenly and finally that my time of playing with buttons was past, just as one summer evening a year or two later, when I had found a perfect slingshot fork in the top of a tree, it came to me that I was no longer interested in slingshots, and I climbed down and left the perfect fork uncut.

I got out the catalogue and looked at the farm equipment, especially the work harness, for I wanted above all things to own my own mule and my own harness. And then I got the paper and read the funnies. But my new knowledge that I had grown beyond playing with buttons had disturbed me, and I was restless.

Seeing that I was, Grandma said, "Why don't you get your horse book and look at it with Grandpa?"

I went and got the book and climbed with it onto Grandpa's lap, something else I was not going to permit myself to do much longer. The book was *The Trotting and Pacing Horse in America* by Hamilton Busby, published in 1904. My father, when he was away at law school, had bought the book and sent it home to Grandpa. I doubt that it had ever mattered much to him, for he was not a man who went much to books for anything, but it mattered a great deal to me. Though the passages on breeders, breeding, and pedigrees meant little to me and I skipped them, by then I was familiar with its many photographs, which I had looked at again and again, and I had practically memorized a few stories of great horses and great races.

It was a book about a kind of glory: the glory of preeminent horses. A horse hitched to any kind of horse-drawn vehicle, by now, is to most people the veriest symbol of obsolescence, and so it comes a little hard to think of the standardbred horse as a phenomenon of the modern world, but that is what he was. His great era was that between the development for general use of smooth-surfaced roads, over which a harness horse could travel at speed, and the mass production of affordable automobiles. At the time of Grandpa's youth and on into his middle years, fast trotters and pacers were in demand. Dan Patch, a bay horse who paced a mile in one minute and fifty-five seconds in 1905, had the reputation of a hero. For a while in his younger days, Grandpa had trained Standardbred horses and had even driven in races in Lexington. He was in Lexington the night they brought the great Dan Patch into the lobby of the Phoenix Hotel. Grandpa did not speak much of these things even to my father, for his own effort ended in disappointment. Hard times came, and he had to give it up. But the passion of it had stayed with him, for it rested upon a passion for good livestock, chiefly horses and mules, that never left him.

There is such a thing as lovesickness for good horses and mules, and for this there is no cure. People who operate machines know nothing like it. This creaturely love can keep one interested all day long in every motion of a good team or a good saddle horse. And not only all day long, but all year round and all life long. Grandpa's life, I think, was shaped around this passion. To him the difference between a good horse or mule and one not so good was paramount, as was the question of how one drove or how one rode.

And so when I climbed into his lap and opened that book, which I believe was the only book that ever had actually belonged to him, and which he probably had not opened for years before I came along and found it and again opened it, I opened a part of his own history that undoubtedly had disappointment in it and pain, and yet I called forth his old passion too, and so he indulged me. Without his small-lensed glasses that he rarely used and probably could not have found, he could not see to read. But I turned through the book from picture to picture, and as his finger came to rest under each one I read off the name of the horse: Lou Dillon, Major Delmar, Dan Patch, Prince Alert, Flora Temple, Dexter, Goldsmith Maid, Nancy Hanks. At that point, for reasons unknown to me then and now, he would exclaim, "Good God A'mighty! Is that Nancy Hanks?" Whatever his reasons, he was moved by his memory of the brown mare who then stood before us, her lead rein held by a man with a mustache wearing a felt hat cocked over his eyes and suspenders over, apparently, a long-sleeved undershirt.

When we had looked at all the pictures, Grandpa put on his coat and cap and overshoes, and, though Grandma said, "Oh, *don't* go out in that old cold wind," I put on mine. We went out to the barn, Grandpa carrying a lighted lantern in one hand and his cane in the other, I walking behind him in the lantern's glow. Our long shadows strode with us, while the starless dark pressed in around us as though to extinguish our light. In the barn we went from stall to stall and into the pen of steers. We looked at every animal. Any one that was lying down Grandpa prodded with the cane, and it got up and stretched and looked at us wide-eyed through the cloud of its breath.

"You want to see them stretch when they get up," Grandpa said. "Then you know they're feeling good. You know they're all right."

This was his requirement for sleep. Knowing that all was well at the barn, he could rest.

On the way back to the house we stood facing away from the wind and took our bedtime pee.

❧

Back in the living room, Grandpa built up the fire for the night, and while I stood close to the stove to get warm again he let down his folding bed and set his chamber pot, his "chamber" as he called it, underneath in its accustomed place. It was bedtime, and he addressed himself to that occasion without any ceremony whatsoever. He stripped off his clothes down to his long underwear and shirt, laid down on his side beneath the covers, rested his head on his turned-back forearm, and closed his eyes. If President and Mrs. Roosevelt had been there, Grandma said, Grandpa would have done the same thing exactly. Long before daylight he would be up again, even if now, in his old age, it would be only to dress, renew the fire, and go to sleep again in his rocking chair.

Grandma blew out one of the lamps and picked up the other. We went through the shadows out into the cold front hall, up the stairs, and into the room over the living room. Grandma set the lamp on the washstand. I put down my grip and, standing over the register that let some heat come up from the stove, I began to take off my clothes.

That reminded Grandma and she said, "Did you brush your teeth, Andy?"

I said, "I don't need to, I don't reckon."

We both knew that was a fib, but the pitcher on the washstand was empty and it was a long way to the kitchen, and so we both pretended that I didn't need to.

I didn't tell her that my pajamas were in my grip. The room was cold and it would be colder in the morning, and so I left on my shirt and long underwear, like Grandpa.

Grandma turned back the covers, I sank into the feather bed, and she covered me up, adding another quilt from the closet. I was so pressed upon from all sides that I didn't think I could move.

Grandma said, "You're snug as a bug in a rug." She said, "Go to sleep, now." And that reminded her of a scrap of eloquence she loved, and she repeated it: "Sleep is nature's sweet restorer." I was a long time learning that she was quoting from Edward Young's *Night Thoughts*. But where had she learned it?

She kissed me goodnight then, picked up the lamp, and went out. She closed the door, perfecting the dark, and I heard her footsteps cross the hall.

We had made little enough of a stir all the evening, but now as we settled for the night the quiet of the empty rooms began to seep into the occupied ones. The old house clicked and ticked in the nighttime cold, and the wind, I thought, was trying to wrap all the way around the walls. In that house, especially in winter, you never forgot the weather. There was no insulation in those days, no double-glazed windows. Only the two rooms were heated. The others, except for hearth fires at special times, stayed cold. And you could hear the wind. My earliest dreams that I remember were dreams of the wind, dreamed in that house.

At first the bed was ice-cold. But I began, gradually and deliciously, to get warm. When I was fully warm, I slept.

❧

I slept the sort of sleep that seems not to have happened. It seemed that I shut my eyes in the room unwalled by darkness and at one with the great night, and promptly opened them again to bright daylight, sunlight beyond the windows, and Grandpa's forefinger prodding me through the covers. He was wearing his cap and his sheepskin coat.

"Wake up, baby," he said in a tone of grief, for I was in violation of his fundamental law. "It's daylight, and you laying there with the sun shining in your eyes!"

His accusation and the broad light did fill me with a sort of panic, for I had not meant to lose a minute of this day, and I had already lost what I knew he considered the best part of it.

All of a sudden I felt ashamed. I knew he was right. I threw off the covers and got up. As I stood over the register again, putting on my clothes, I heard him going down the stairs and back through the house. He had a determined, final way of walking, as if he were leaving his footprints in the floors. He made things rattle.

Dressing didn't take me long. Grandma, I think, had not wanted me to be waked up, and she and Grandpa had exchanged some words on the matter. When I came into the kitchen Grandma was saying, "Yes, I reckon you would," but he was already out the door.

Since I was up and there was no helping it, she set about my breakfast.

"Wash up," she said. "It'll be ready in a minute."

It wasn't long until I was eating fried eggs, a fried slice of the Christmas ham, hot biscuits and peach preserves, and a glass of milk that Grandma kept refilling before I had emptied it.

"Could I have one more egg and two more biscuits?"

"You can have all you want," she said.

When I was finished, she struck a blow for civilization by making me brush my teeth. And then she made me go out to the privy, though I would have preferred constipation to that cold seat. And then she made me go through the motions of combing my hair.

As soon as I had met all her requirements, I went straight to the stripping room. The work was continuing as before, but Fred, who I had hoped would be there, was not. His mother must have needed him at home.

Who was there was Uncle Jack Beechum, my great-great-uncle on my mother's side and Grandpa's neighbor. Uncle Jack—or "Old Jack," as he had come to call himself and as he was called—was four years older than Grandpa and would survive him by six years. But they were contemporaries, old friends, and they knew the same things. The presence of the two of them together had an influence on the room and made it quieter. While they talked, even Rufus Brightleaf listened and said not much. Uncle Jack was as tall as Grandpa, but whereas

Grandpa was lean and hard-fleshed, Uncle Jack, though by no means fat, was stoutly built—"a draft horse of a man," Grandpa called him. And whereas Grandpa's voice was edged as though he spoke determinedly on his own authority, Uncle Jack's voice came rumbling up out of his big chest as though he pronounced on behalf of a deliberative body. He had walked over that morning to learn how the work was going, which he had promptly seen for himself, and he lingered now to talk.

Uncle Jack was a widower, keeping house for himself in the manner of an old man not much interested in keeping house. Like Grandpa, he had become dependent on other people to keep his place going. Because he was not easily satisfied, he was never satisfied with the tenants who so far had come one year and, not satisfying, gone the next. Because he respected the Brightleafs, he wanted to know if they knew of anybody who was "the right kind." The right kind, never plentiful, were scarcer than ever. Jess and Rufus could only say that they would be on the lookout.

Uncle Jack forsook his present worries, and the conversation, belonging then to him and Grandpa, took up the burden of times only they had known. They spoke of horses and mules and men and days. Now I can wish that I had stayed and listened and tried to remember. Now I can wish I had foreseen then what I would want to know now, and had asked the questions I now wish I had asked. What did their elders remember of the Civil War, and of the time before that? What did they tell about slavery? After the war, how were things rearranged between the races? Was the Klan active here? What did it do? Who was in it? What was it like here before the railroad came, or all-weather roads, when the only dependable transportation to and from Port William was by the river? What did they remember of the then still-standing ancient forests? How did they make it through the depression of the 1890s? The drouth of 1908? But a boy's mind is different from an old man's by precisely a lifetime. And so the talk of that day went out into that day's air and light and the silence beyond, and the silence has kept it.

Grandpa and Uncle Jack were sitting on the only two five-gallon buckets in the room, leaving me no place to sit, or even stand, where I would be out of the way. If Jess Brightleaf had only given me some little bit of work to do, some way of helping, I would gladly have paid him both my dollars. But it was not to be, and I knew it. And so I had nothing to do, no part in the talk, and no place to stand where I would not be told to move.

Pitching my voice low so as not to seem to interrupt my elders, I said, "Where's Fred?"

"He went to shit and the hogs eat him," said Rufus Brightleaf. It was not an unfriendly remark, but it did not encourage further conversation on my part.

Outside the sun was shining, and I went out.

The stripping room was the wrong place for me that day, but it has stayed luminous in my mind as it was then: a place of order, of fine work, of the fragrance of cured tobacco, of the beautiful browns of the graded leaves in the discriminate north light. And I can see its population of that morning as clearly as if I were still standing at the door, ready to leave: Jess Brightleaf, whose mind made the order and set the standard of the work, less by any word than by the mere force of his presence; Rufus Brightleaf palavering loosely of the sins and pleasures of the flesh but in fact caring and capable enough to satisfy even his brother; Dick Watson patiently doing as he needed to do; Old Man Hawk, who had the power of silence and of not caring; and the two old neighbors dreaming and talking of times long gone. And all around, beyond the happenstance of that quiet place, was the whole world at war, forgettable from moment to moment, but recallable at any instant by somebody's naming of one of the absent or one of the dead.

In my memory all who were there, except for Old Man Hawk, seem now to be gathered into a love that is at once a boy's and an aging man's — and also, I think, into a love older and larger that is grieved, amused, grateful, and merciful. Only Old Man Hawk seems to belong to nobody's love. He stood alone on his own small dignity that did not condescend even to work as well as he could have. He did not give a damn. He took what he wanted of what was available. He would in fact steal a chicken, and had done so. He would in fact kill a man, and had done so. The only reason he was not a liar was that he didn't talk enough.

I went out and Rufus came after me, grinning, to see that I didn't do what I had done before and was likely to do again.

"Andy, don't fasten that damned door on the outside, now."

I didn't. As I left I heard him fasten it on the inside.

The day was bright and cold, the ground hard frozen. I went down the hill, crossing a swag, and a little ways up again to where Dick and Aunt Sarah Jane's house sat at the corner of the woods. I let myself through the yard gate by the water maple

Dick had planted, that was getting almost big enough to cast a useful shade, and went up to the door and knocked. Dick's old foxhound, Waxy, had come out from under the house to be petted and now she waited with me at the door, though she would not be let in.

Aunt Sarah Jane greeted me, made me welcome, and asked me to take a chair, all with some ceremony. She was a woman of impeccable manners, in her fashion a lady of the old school. She was affable, talkative, always ready to cut loose with a big laugh, but with a reserve of dignity too that kept me conscious of my own manners. I never let her see the impudence I sometimes displayed to Grandma.

We sat in rocking chairs on either side of the drum stove. The house was warm and full of the morning sunlight. It was a small house, only two rooms, but tightly built, ceiled on the inside with tongue and groove. One of the rooms was the kitchen. The one we were sitting in was both bedroom and living room. This room, like the other, was crowded with furniture, including a quilting frame with a quilt on it. In spite of her arthritic hands and aging eyes, Aunt Sarah Jane was a seamstress and was always at work with needle and thimble, repairing or patching or making something useful and pretty.

She reckoned I had had a nice Christmas. She spoke of the birth of the baby Jesus with such immediacy of imagination that it might have happened only five nights ago in our own barn. She required me to tell her how I was and how all of my family were. And then she told me her news, nearly all of which had taken place within the radius of eyesight from her windows and yard, or within her mind. It concerned the doings of weather, animals, and people, and also several biblical characters, remembered people, and ghosts. All the creatures she knew, living and dead, natural and supernatural, were to her immediately present. Her mind was yeasty, full of knowledge, and always at work. Some of the things she knew would have seemed exceedingly doubtful to a skeptic, which I was not. The world, as she knew it, was not fenced around with facts or proofs or conventions of "objective truth." She told of what she had *seen*. She had seen ghosts. She had seen the devil. She had seen people dancing in the street at the end of World War I with the Kaiser's head on a pole. She had seen snakes of kinds, sizes, colors, and habits that astounded me, and would have astounded a herpetologist too.

For my part, I was then not so much superstitious as merely and totally gullible, able to believe without a grain of doubt anything whatever that was told me by anybody older than I was. And my imagination was capable of ratifying the wildest errors and my own most extravagant misunderstandings. When I was in the first grade, the doctor who served as the county's "health officer" entered our classroom and announced that he had come to look for head lice. He then went up and down the rows of desks, parting the students' hair with his fingers and looking. But I had misheard him; I thought he said he had come to look for *headlights*. And it seemed all at once credible and wonderful to me that some of us might have lights in the tops of our heads, hidden by our hair. Another time, I heard my father tell my mother at breakfast, "I heard wild geese flying over last night," but I thought he said he had heard wild *beasts* flying over. I had a book of pictures of African animals, and my misunderstanding gave me a vision of winged zebras, giraffes, and lions flying over our house in the night. Their wings stroked the air with a stately motion, and their eyes were fixed upon the distance with a solemnity that seemed heroic and holy. They seemed perfectly believable to me, for I could *see* them. I can see them yet.

And so in those days my mind was perfectly compatible with Aunt Sarah Jane's. Everything that was vivid and wondrously true to her was vivid and wondrously true to me. Everything she told me fell upon my consciousness like seeds upon fertile ground.

But not everything she told me came from the realm of wonder. She also spoke that day, as she often did, of the rights that her people had been promised but had never been given. She was my first preceptor in the matters of race and civil rights. Because I always listened attentively to her, everything she said struck in. She made me feel responsible, for I knew, as she required me to know, that I was a product of my culture; but I felt it vaguely, for I could not precisely locate in myself the cause of the injury. I had no ill will toward her or Dick, or in fact toward any of the black people I knew, and besides, if I were greatly to blame, why was she so nice to me?

Both the sense of responsibility and the perhaps necessary vagueness have stayed with me until now. Starting probably with those conversations so long ago with Aunt Sarah Jane, I have learned to understand the old structure of racism as a malevolent convention, the malevolence of which is hard to locate in the conscious intentions of most people. It was a circumstance that was mostly taken for granted. It was inexcusable, and yet we had the formidable excuse of being used to it. It was an injustice both accommodated and varyingly obscured not only by daily custom, but also by the exigencies and preoccupations of daily life. We left the issue alone, not exactly by ignoring it, but by observing an elaborate etiquette that permitted us to ignore it. White people who wished to think well of themselves did not use the language of racial insult in front of black people. But the problem for us white people, as we had finally to understand, was that we could not be selectively complicit. To be complicit at all, even thoughtlessly by custom, was to be complicit in the whole extent and reach of the injustice. It is hard for a customary indifference to unstick itself from the abominations to which it tacitly consents. But we were used to it. What is hardest to get used to maybe, once you are aware, is the range of things humans are able to get used to. I was more used to this once than I am now.

Aunt Sarah Jane's plain talk of racial injustice as she knew it, thereby introducing the fester of it into the conscience of a small boy, who knew it only as the accepted way and a mandatory etiquette, was by the measure of that time remarkable. To the extent that her talk was a discomfort and an instruction, it was a service. To the extent that it was interesting and a part of conversation, it was hospitality. Her conversation could sometimes be the wildest mixture of sense and what I still regret to call superstition. I listened to her with the keenest interest, sometimes with a kind of awe, and sometimes with a fearful eagerness, trying to penetrate even a little some mystery that she spoke of or from.

By her charity, good cheer, and love of company, it was eminently pleasant to sit with her in that warm room, mindful of the cold outside, mostly listening and asking questions while she followed her thoughts along their wandering paths, now and then renewing the bolus of snuff that she kept inside her lower lip, or making use of her "spit can."

She sang me a song in which a young man, plowing corn, dreams of Saturday night:

> Diddle-um, diddle-um, di-de-o,
> Gon' take Sal to the party-o.
> Haw, Lige!

"But, Aunt Sarah Jane, who's Lige?"
"Why honey, Lige was his *mule!*"
I would gladly go back to sit with her again. She too I loved. She too is a knot in the net that has gathered me up and kept me alive until now.

❧

From Aunt Sarah Jane's I went straight out to the mailbox and then to Grandma's kitchen. I didn't go by the stripping room even to see if Fred had come with his mother to bring dinner. The stripping room part of my visit seemed to be over, and I didn't want to go back.

Grandpa was already at the table when I came into the kitchen with the mail. We had another good dinner, pretty much like the one of the day before, ending with the rest of the raspberry pie. Afterwards, instead of going back outside, I stayed with Grandma. I helped her to do the dishes and tidy up the kitchen, and I brought in a fresh bucket of water from the well.

When we got everything put to rights, we went into the living room. She took up her needlework. I read the funnies, and then returned to *The Boy's King Arthur*. I opened it to the beginning. I looked at the words and I could hear my mother's voice reading

them, and so as I looked from word to word I too was reading
them:

> *And when the first mass was done there was seen in the church-*
> *yard, against the high altar, a great stone four-square, like to a*
> *marble stone, and in the midst thereof was an anvil of steel, a*
> *foot of height, and therein stuck a fair sword naked by the point,*
> *and letters of gold were written about the sword that said thus:*
> Who so pulleth out this sword of this stone and anvil, is
> right-wise king born of England.

I didn't know what a mass was, but it didn't seem to matter
much. I knew very well what an anvil was, but I couldn't figure
out the need for an anvil *and* a stone. I thought either one would
have been plenty.

But I was reading, and it was my mother's voice that was
sounding in my mind as I read. Since I had learned so far no respect
for sequence, and anyhow we had already got well into the book,
I skipped over to the quarrel between Sir Launcelot and Queen
Guenever, and still my mother's voice continued, and still I read:

> *"Alas!" said Sir Bors, "that ever Sir Launcelot's kin saw you. For*
> *now have ye lost the best knight of our blood, and he that was*
> *all our leader and our succor. And I dare say and make it good,*
> *that all kings, Christian nor heathen, may not find such a knight,*
> *for to speak of his nobleness and courtesy with his beauty and*
> *his gentleness. "Alas," said Sir Bors, "what shall we do that be*
> *of his blood?"*
> *"Alas!" said Sir Ector de Maris.*
> *"Alas!" said Sir Lionel.*

૩ૠ

When I was behaving myself and out of trouble more or less everywhere, my mother was a refuge to me. She understood the not always manifest quietness I had inside me that made me dislike gatherings and want to be alone. Even when it put her at her wit's end, she understood it. She understood my times of introspection and silence, my susceptibility of being carried away by a book or a thought or something vividly seen in my mind. She encouraged my intermittent bookishness. She approved of what she called my "long thoughts." She was often only amused at my weakness for drifting away from whatever I was supposed to be doing—except when I was supposed to be doing my homework. When I drifted away—mentally or (as I preferred) physically—from that, I "drove her crazy" and made her wonder what was going to become of me. There were times when I sat helplessly not-thinking about my math while she stood over me as helplessly, and perhaps hopelessly too, with a shingle or a switch. At my best, I hope, I deserved her sympathy, for I greatly needed it and took shelter in it. She was, and her memory is, a comfort to me.

Though the thought of him is a comfort to me now, my father then seemed to me an eminence, a distant height, even when he was holding me by the hand or in his lap. That he also was and would be a refuge I never doubted. But his love was proprietary, like Grandma's; it was magisterial, fierce, and demanding. When he hugged me, he hugged me tight, with an urgency just short of violence, as if foreseeing the times when he would be unable to decide for me or protect me, as if it were an immediate, almost a maternal, grief to him that we were not one flesh. Whereas I was slow in my thoughts, dreamy, and clumsy, he was all concentrated energy and attention, competent, purposeful, efficient in act and speech. When I would be gaping at some vision or actual sight while the sheep I should have headed bolted and the others followed, he would say, "There you stand, Andy, looking out your mouth!" His hands were strong, capable, and utterly direct. When he would catch me using awkwardly a broom or a shovel, he would take hold of me and it and correct my stance and movements, as if under some irresistible compulsion to remold the too-watery clay of which I was made.

And so on this solitary journey of mine, I was experiencing my absence from my father with a relish that I could not then have defined, and I was beginning to miss my mother and the sound of my mother's voice a little more than I would have cared to admit.

My mother I believe I knew fairly well from a fairly early age. Looking back, I love her simply as I knew her to be. And I wonder, too, at what she came to be as she grew older and the trials of motherhood and other early difficulties fell away from her. In her old age she seemed to me to become almost purely generous and wise. Unlike my father, for whom love was always involved with fear and exasperation and who felt personally affronted by any unremedied flaw, she accepted what she could not help and came finally to a quietness within herself that signified great faith, and no fear at all.

But I had to grow and age into knowledge of my father, and I am afraid to say yet that I know him fairly well. Insofar as he was a critic of the people and places he loved, he was as much a visionary all his life as ever I was to be at any age—though at the age of nine I could not have envisioned *that*. He bore the burden of his certainty that some things could be improved, and of his vision of how to improve them. And over and over again he suffered enormous frustration at his or anybody's inability to make the needed correction.

Both he and my mother were motivated by great love, but hers abounded quietly, and his was instant and ungraduated, always at full flow.

One morning as I was watching him shave, I asked experimentally, "Daddy, what would you do if I died?"

His reply was shocking, for it came while the sound of my voice seemed still in the air, and with a force of passion that I had not until then imagined: "I would cry my eyes out!"

❧

"Well, you're a great one for a book," my father's mother said to me as we sat long ago by the stove in her living room. Like my father, she was rarely satisfied with things as they were. If I was reading, she recognized that as a good thing, but then she would be obliged to suspect that I might be reading too much, or the wrong kind of book, or that there might be something else I ought to be doing. For she too was a critic, though a companionable one when you were on her safe side.

She called me back, it seemed, from far away, as it seems she can still call me back from so far in time. I looked up from the book and was happy to see that I was there with her.

"You go upstairs and get your grip," she said, "and put all your things in it. So you'll be ready when your granddaddy comes to get you. He'll be here before long."

I had forgotten about that. I was still a traveler. I was going to stay the next two nights with my mother's parents, Granny and Granddaddy Feltner, in Port William. The happiness of traveling by myself came upon me again. There was more to look forward to.

I brought down my grip, stuck my book in on top of my clothes, found my toothbrush and stuck it in. Except for putting on my wraps, I was ready.

"I guess I'm ready," I said.

"Well, your old grandma hates to see you go," Grandma said. "We'll miss you when you're gone."

That made me realize that I hated to go. I would miss them when I was gone. To make a journey, especially alone, always carries a metaphorical power, and I felt the sorrow of it pass over me. We come to a place we love, we meet loved ones there, and we go. The thought of leaving made me realize how much I liked being there with her. I looked around for something more to do, something she and I could do, before I would have to go.

I took down from the top of Grandpa's folding bed the pretty candy box filled with picture postcards and photographs that were Grandma's precious keepsakes. There weren't many of either, of course. She had never owned a camera, and so the photographs all had been sent to her. And the people we were kin to did not often make trips from which they sent postcards. But all the pictures and cards had names and brought forth stories. This place had been home to kinfolk and others who had moved away, and who wrote back, trying to maintain a connection that over the years grew weaker. Grandma was a faithful keeper of their memories. We spoke then of the absent and the dead. Our talk took on the charm of distance and history almost like the stories of King Arthur and the knights of the Round Table. But this was *our* history and these were *our* people. Their names and stories and pictures had a worth to us that was timely and bodily and never to be put in a book.

After a while we saw Granddaddy Feltner's old green Plymouth turn in at the gate and come up the driveway and past the house. He would leave the car in the barn lot and come to the back door, and so I picked up my grip and we went out to the kitchen to meet him.

I was still getting into my wraps when Grandma opened the kitchen door and Granddaddy came in smiling and asking if they had a boy there who needed a ride to Port William. He said the boy was a traveler by the name of Andy Catlett.

I laughed and ran to hug him, and he said, "Hello, son."

He and Grandma exchanged greetings and a little news. And then, in spite of all I could do, Grandma buttoned up my mackinaw for me and pulled my toboggan well down over my ears. She hugged me and kissed me and said, "Come back soon," as if I might never return.

I said, "I'll be back."

And then Granddaddy picked up my grip and took my hand, and we went out.

III

Granddaddy Feltner was younger by nineteen years than Grandpa Catlett, and this difference made other differences. Granddaddy owned a car and could drive it, and thus, unlike Grandpa, he had come consciously into the era of internal combustion. Though I was a conservative child, whose heart was given more finally than I knew to the creaturely world of Grandpa Catlett, it seemed perfectly normal to me also to be driving back along the ridges toward Port William with Granddaddy Feltner in his car. The car was older than I was, and the war would have to end before it could be replaced with a new one. Like the team and wagon, it seemed to belong to the world that I belonged to.

And yet the world that I belonged to was already divided, as I have said, into two opposing worlds, the sun-powered world of horse and mule teams, and the petroleum-powered world of cars and trucks and tractors. As I look back into my memory, where hindsight now seems strangely mixed with foreknowledge, I can see doom clearly written upon the older world, though I believe that the whole cost of that doom is still unpaid.

Granddaddy's old car would seem crude to us now in "the new millennium." It was crude in comparison even to my father's car, which was newer. But on that day, having returned to motor travel from my trip with Dick and Grandpa in the wagon, and after nearly two days of getting about on foot, I felt the car's ease and speed. We were effortlessly and in just minutes covering a distance that had seemed long to me the morning before.

And I noticed something else. The car was not only easier and faster than the team and wagon. It gave a new aspect and a new motion to the world. The wagon passed through the country at a speed that allowed your eyes to come to rest. Whatever you wanted to look at in the road ditch or the fencerow or the field beyond, your sight could dwell on and you could see it. But from the side window of Granddaddy's car where I was looking out, the country seemed to be turning by like a great wheel. The rim of the wheel, at the roadside, was turning so fast that everything was a blur. To pick out a detail — one fencepost, one rock, one tree trunk — was impossible. The effort to do so made me feel cross-eyed and kind of sick. Farther away, the wheel turned more slowly and you could look at things, you could stop them in your eyes, but the smaller details were getting lost. Even farther away, as if near the wheel's hub, things seemed hardly to be moving, but there were no details at all, just the vague blue ridges way off there as if in a different world. And that, as I now know, would be the new world, the "world of the future," which to most people in it would be hazy and without detail, way off in the distance.

By fortune of birth and history, I know the world of horses and mules that lived on a while into my time. I know also the world of the automobile, which excluded the older world by means of speed, comfort, and ease, and which oddly "made the world smaller" by increasing the distances between ourselves and the things we need. And like many others in this rational modern age, I have sat in airplanes going five hundred miles an hour and wished they would hurry up.

Granddaddy would often carry on a little foolishness to amuse himself or me, but he was not a jabberer.

When we started out, he said, "Hon, have you got everything you brought? You didn't forget anything?"

And I replied with my best manners, "No, sir."

And then, when we came into Port William: "Well, here we are. Home again."

"Yes, sir."

The Feltner house, where Uncle Virgil and my mother and Granddaddy too had been raised, stood both at the corner of the little town and at the corner of the farm that had been the Feltner home place time out of mind. The electric lines had come to Port William before I was born, and so Granny and Granddaddy's house had electric lights. It also had bathrooms, and it had "central heating" from a big coal furnace in the basement. It was a brick house of ten rooms, built right on the street in the fashion of all the old town houses in our part of the country, though, unlike most, this one had a large front porch and an ample, tree-shaded yard on each side.

Of all the houses I knew as a child, this one was the most welcoming, not because of its conveniences, which were unusual for the time and place, but because of the generosity of Granny and Granddaddy. I think it had always been a welcoming house. I know it had been so at least as far back as the time of Ben and Nancy Feltner, Granddaddy's parents, long dead but known familiarly still, even to me, as Pa and Ma Feltner. Granny and Granddaddy seem to have inherited the welcoming along with the house. The house, you might say, had the habit of hospitality. In the time of my boyhood, Granny and Granddaddy were always "having company": visiting preachers, relatives, friends of relatives, sometimes utter strangers who were friends of friends of relatives. This custom had survived, pretty well intact, from the time of bad roads when anybody who arrived at mealtime expected, and was expected, to eat, and anybody who came in the evening spent the night.

And so when I came, I came as a grandson, more or less a member of the household, but I came also as company. Company in fact was already there when I came. Granny's sister-in-law, Ora Finley, known to my mother and so to us children as "Auntie," was then with her sister Lizzie Lord, who had been Granny's best friend all their lives, and who, though no kin to us, was known to us as "Aunt Lizzie." They had been there since Christmas Eve. Both were widows by then, both childless, and

they were living together in Auntie's house at Hargrave. Aunt
Lizzie had been Auntie's baby sister. She was still girlish, and
had not altogether ceased to think of herself as a girl. Time and
age and loss, I think, had remained surprising to her. She was
a jolly companion to us children. Auntie, on the contrary, was
strict, stoic, forthright, without a grain of nonsense, and she
had a fine comic sense of the ridiculous. You would know in an
instant that she was a woman who would put up only with so
much, and you would not be eager to find out how much. Her
own childlessness had freed her to assume certain responsibil-
ities for the upbringing of my mother and Uncle Virgil. She
was a lover of books, and she had encouraged that love in my
mother and in me.

And Hannah was there. She had lived there with Uncle Virgil
after they married, and she would continue to live there, after
Uncle Virgil's death in the war and the birth of their daughter,
until she married again in 1948.

When Granddaddy took me in, like company, through the
front door, there they were, lined up in the hall like a welcoming
committee: Granny and Auntie and Aunt Lizzie and Hannah.

"Well, look who's here!" Granny said, opening her arms.
"Come here and hug your granny!"

I went down the line, getting hugged and kissed and exclaimed
over until I was as spoiled already as I would be when I got home
and would overhear my mother saying to Granny on the telephone, "Oh, yes, I'm glad to have him back, even if you have
spoiled him rotten."

When I got to Hannah she gave me a smile and a hug without

saying anything, for she was not an exclaiming woman. And she put a kiss on my cheek that stayed there until she gave me another one just as good at bedtime that night.

☙

Though the Feltner house was far more modern in its appliances than that of my Catlett grandparents, the same household economy of home production and diligent thrift prevailed there also. Everything that the place could provide, it did provide, and in abundance. Like Grandma Catlett, Granny Feltner still made her own lye soap for the washing of dishes and clothes.

I think often now of that old economy, which was essentially the same from a farm household that was fairly well-to-do, like that of Granny and Granddaddy Feltner, to the household of Dick Watson and Aunt Sarah Jane, which would be classified as poor. For many years now that way of living has been scorned, and over the last forty or fifty years it has nearly disappeared. Even so, there was nothing wrong with it. It was an economy directly founded on the land, on the power of the sun, on thrift and skill, and on the people's competence to take care of themselves. They had become dependent, to some extent, on manufactured goods, but as long as they stayed on their farms and made use of the great knowledge that they possessed, they could have survived foreseeable calamities that their less resourceful descendants could not survive. Now that we have come to the end of the era of cheap petroleum, which fostered so great a forgetfulness, I see that we could have continued that thrifty old life fairly comfortably — could even have improved it. Now we will have to return to it, or to a life necessarily as careful, and we will do so only uncomfortably and with much distress.

Increasingly over the last maybe forty years, the thought has come to me that the old world in which our people lived by the work of their hands, close to weather and earth, plants and animals, was the true world; and that the new world of cheap energy and ever cheaper money, honored greed, and dreams of liberation from every restraint, is mostly theater. This new world seems a jumble of scenery and props never quite believable, an economy of fantasies and moods, in which it is hard to remember either the timely world of nature or the eternal world of the prophets and poets. And I fear, I believe I know, that the doom of the older world I knew as a boy will finally afflict the new one that replaced it.

The world I knew as a boy was flawed, surely, but it was substantial and authentic. The households of my grandparents seemed to breathe forth a sense of the real cost and worth of things. Whatever came, came by somebody's work.

While I was preoccupied with being greeted and then with sitting in the living room with the women, who wanted to be told how everybody was at home when I left and how I had enjoyed my trip and what all I had done out at Grandma and Grandpa's, Granddaddy had disappeared. As I replied to the women's questions, much apparently to their pleasure and much therefore to my own, my mind nevertheless was increasingly troubled by the feeling that I was missing something.

I knew where Granddaddy had gone. He was out amongst the farm buildings and the livestock, helping his lifelong hired hand and friend from boyhood, Joe Banion, do up the evening chores. And finally I needed to get out of the center of attention. I didn't want to hear myself say any more about where I had been and what I had done. It is the responsibility of a traveler to tell stories, but enough is enough.

I said, "I think I ought to go see where Granddaddy is."

"Don't do that now," Granny said. "It's not long till supper. No use tracking around in the mud and manure for nothing."

That gave me another thought. "Can I go tell Uncle Ernest supper's about ready?"

"*May* I go," Auntie said, standing in for my mother and my teacher.

I almost said "Sure." I got right to the edge of that cliff before I caught myself. I said, "May I go tell Uncle Ernest?"

"He'll know when it's supper time," Granny said. "But you can go to the shop and walk back with him if you want to."

Once I was outdoors in the quiet, I recovered the sense of myself as a solitary traveler. It came to me that, starting from the tracks I stood in, there in front of the old house, I could have gone anywhere. But I was going to Uncle Ernest's shop because that was where Granny was expecting me to go, and it was where I wanted to go. Uncle Ernest was Granny's youngest brother, a man fascinating to Henry and me because of his work and because of the long stories he would tell us, lasting, some of them, through the bedtimes of two weeks.

I crossed the road and turned into the alley between the hotel and the post office. Uncle Ernest's shop was back at the end of the alley, sort of unlooked-at, out on the edge of things. His old pickup truck was parked in front, where it stayed most of the time in the winter. Smoke was coming out of the chimney. I opened the door and stepped into the warmth and the good smells.

Uncle Ernest was working at the bench, his crutches propped against the wall out of the way. When he heard me come in, he looked around and said, "Hello, Andy."

"Uncle Ernest," I said, "it won't be long till supper."

"I figured it was getting about that time."

He had a way of talking to boys as if they were grown men. He only treated you like a child if you were being childish, and then it was awful. You knew without being told that there were limits to what he would put up with. He was like Auntie in that way.

He had been badly hurt in the First World War. Being crippled had changed him and changed his life, but there were limits also to his acceptance of his handicap. He would work mostly back there in his shop during the winter, repairing things, making things, refinishing furniture. He was handy. He could do anything he set his hands to. He kept everybody's clocks running. He could fix the electrical household gadgets that were coming more and more into use. But his great gift and his passion were for wood, and the shop was filled with the smells of newly worked lumber, of shellac, varnish, paint, and glue. It was as fragrant in its way, as inviting and tempting, as a kitchen. It gave forth also the sounds of hammers, hatchets, drawknives, spokeshaves, saws, augers, planes, rasps, sandpaper. It was full of tools curious and beautiful to the eye, the metal polished and the handles lustrous from use. They were beautiful in themselves, in use, and in Uncle Ernest's mastery of them.

The smells and sounds and sights of the place summoned a boy to come close, to take part, to help. But the shop was above all orderly, clean as a pin, and everything he wasn't using would be in its place. There were rules also, three of them, that applied to boys: Don't touch, Stand back, Be quiet. They were good rules, for they set the terms of Uncle Ernest's welcome to boys that was genuine and generous. If you asked him, "What're you making?" he would answer without looking at you, "Layos to catch meddlers." But if you kept quiet and watched, you would see what he was making. If after a while you couldn't figure it out, he would know it. He would say, "Do you know what I'm making?" and you would say, "No." And then he would explain patiently and clearly. Sometimes he would say, "Do you want to try your hand at this?" and you would say, "Yes." And then he would show you how.

From the time the weather got good in the spring until it turned cold again, he worked outdoors. And the shop also contained, in their places against the wall, the ladders, jacks, and other equipment that he would need then. Some work was too heavy for him, but people generally knew what he was capable of, and he seldom had to refuse a job. It was surprising what he could do. He used the crutches when he had any distance to walk. But when he started to work he put them aside, though he did look horribly crippled then, and he did not like people to watch him. He worked mainly alone. But if he thought of himself as a cripple, he was too proud to let you know it, even though nearly all the Port William men called him "Crip" and he answered to the name. His arms and upper body were powerful, as you would expect, and he made perhaps merciless demands upon his poor legs. He could carry a considerable load up a ladder. He could replace the siding on a barn. One time Martin Rowanberry came upon him sitting flat on the ground, cutting down a big tree with an axe. Mart himself told me this long after Uncle Ernest was dead. Mart said he was a good axeman. He never wasted a lick. The big chips were flying.

I stood at the appointed distance and watched him, neither of us saying anything more. He was replacing a leg on somebody's table. It was a ticklish job, involving mortises, tenons, and pegs.

After a while, still attentive to his work, he said, "I don't reckon you're looking forward to supper."

And I said, as I was supposed to, "I don't reckon so."

He worked on a few moments more, and then he put his tools away. He brushed the accumulated dust and shavings off the bench and swept them into a neat pile on the floor. They would help the stove to get hot early the next morning. Finished, then, he turned to me and smiled.

"Well, you may not be hungry, but I am. Let's go."

He got his crutches and I went ahead of him out the door.

☙

Supper at Granny Feltner's was a sort of indoor picnic of cold leftovers and sandwich makings. Nettie Banion, Granny's cook, would have gone down through the field to her own house after the dinner dishes were done, and supper was meant to be an easy meal that did not heat up the kitchen in the summertime or leave cooking utensils to be washed. Under the bright electric light, that evening of my arrival, Granny and Hannah had laid out the rest of the Christmas ham and turkey on their platters, and mayonnaise and cranberry sauce, and a plate of cold biscuits and a loaf of Granny's salt-rising bread to make sandwiches with, and a pitcher of milk. There was a pot of coffee hot on the stove for whoever wanted it. For dessert there was fruit cake and jam cake and custard with whipped cream. And in the refrigerator, especially for me, was a tray of ice cream made with cream from the Jersey cows. "Save room," Granny said when she told me about it.

To me, the kitchen always bespoke the presence of Nettie Banion, even when she was absent from it, as it bespoke also the presence of Aunt Fanny, who had been there when my mother was young, and of Aunt Cass, who had been there when Granddaddy was young. All three in their times had married Banion men, Smoke and Samp and Joe, and all three had come up the hill to this house in the early mornings to cook breakfast and dinner, to help with the housework, and then had gone back home to keep house and fix supper in that other life that we white people knew existed but did not know.

When I was staying in Port William and Granny had something to say to me that was especially important, she would make me a little speech. This was because of my mind's bad reputation for wandering. That night, after we had eaten our supper and were dawdling at the table, Granny said:

"Andy, listen to Granny for a minute. I know you want to go downtown to see if any of your friends are there. And that's all right. But I want you to be back here at eight o'clock. Now, what did I say?"

I said, "I can go downtown, but I have to be back by eight o'clock. Well, I would like to. But how am I going to know when it's eight o'clock?"

"There'll be people down there who'll know," she said. "Just tell somebody to tell you when it's time."

"Yes, mam."

And so she freed me and bound me at the same time, something she was good at.

✿

I set forth again into the town of Port William, the nucleus, the navel, of the country that was most intimately home to me then and has been home to me all my life, even in the years when I did not live in it. It is my motherland, the mold I was cast in. As it has held and shaped me, so I have kept and contained it. Though I may have been thousands of miles away, it has been as present to me as my own flesh.

The town of Hargrave, where I was living then, had been infected perhaps from the beginning with the modern ambition to be what it was not. It longed, as people say now, to realize its full potential, whatever that might be. But Port William was eagerly interested in itself, interminably telling itself its own stories.

Of Port William proper, the center, there never has been much: a scattering of houses along the road, a church, a school, a graveyard, and what in a bigger town would have been the "business district," which was my destination. In those days Port William's business district consisted of two general stores, Milton Burgess's and Jasper Lathrop's, Jasper's being closed at the time because Jasper was in the army; a still-working blacksmith shop; a garage and car dealership, the life of which coincided just about exactly with the working life of Mr. Milo Settle; Dolph Courtney's "drug store," which sold patent medicines, ice cream, "notions and sundries," and comic books; the Port William branch of The Independent Farmer's Bank; Uncle Ernest's woodworking shop; Jayber Crow's barbershop; a pool room; the paintless hotel, which now offered room and board mainly to old people; and the post office. Now we have perhaps a few more houses than then, but only one general store, an "antique and junque" store, the bank, and the post office. The Port William School of eight grades, which was going strong in 1943, has been shut now for forty years.

I knew several Port William boys about my age, with whom I played or rambled when I visited Granny and Granddaddy, and I was on the lookout for them. When I went out, all that was left of the day was just a little afterlight in the west. I crossed the street and went by the post office, which was dark; and by the hotel, which was showing a light way in the back where Mrs. Hendrick was serving supper to her boarders; by the blacksmith shop, where there was a basketball goal in the cindery lot in front; and by Jasper Lathrop's store, which was shut and dark. Dolph Courtney's store was showing a little light, but nobody was in there, and so Dolph had turned off all the lights except one naked bulb over the ice cream counter, on which Dolph was leaning, reading the paper. It was too dark to make out the covers of the comic books he had on display in the front window.

When I got to the poolroom, I stood and thought awhile about going in, which I had done a time or two when I was rambling about with Danny Branch and Orvie Galingale. I might have gone in if I had been with them, but I was alone, and moreover I was traveling alone and so was unusually mindful of my responsibility. Things went on in that poolroom, according to Granny, that she did not recommend to boys my age. I was, in fact, strictly forbidden to go in there.

Next was Dr. Markman's little office of two white-painted, board-walled rooms. He was still busy, for there was a light on in the back room and his old car was parked in front. It was a coupe of some kind, black by the manufacturer's intention, but in fact mostly the color of mud: of dried mud until it rained, and then the color of wet mud. Sometimes his patients visited him in his office. More often he called upon them, driving the creek roads and the farm tracks at all hours, carrying a few instruments and bottles of pills in a leather satchel that was as professionally black as it was meant to be. I did not dislike Dr. Markman, but my few encounters with him had not been entirely pleasant, for he came where sickness was. Once, when I got the flu at Granny's house, she called Dr. Markman. He was a good-humored man, and he made us all feel better just by coming into the room with the air of the harsh winter night emanating like an aura from his clothes. But when he applied his cold, hairy ear to my back to listen to my lungs, it felt as big as a dinner plate.

I went on down to the barbershop at the bottom of the swag in the middle of town. Nobody at all was in there. Even Jayber was gone. He had left a light on to show that he was open for business, but everybody probably had got their hair cut right before Christmas, and so he had given up and gone off somewhere. I crossed over to Mr. Settle's garage and went back up the hill to Milton Burgess's store. The lights were on there, and I could see through the window that people were inside, if not customers at least loafers. I went in to see who was there and what there was to see.

The first sight, of course, was Mr. Burgess smiling at me from behind the counter. "Good evening, Mr. Catlett," he said in his official-greeting voice while everybody looked at me. "What can I do for you this evening?"

He sounded ready, if I had only said the word, to stand on his head or jump through a hoop. Nothing could have been more embarrassing. I said, "Not anything, I don't reckon."

"Not anything it will be then," said Mr. Burgess, grinning at me through his spectacles and rapping a little tattoo on the counter with his fingers.

Somebody laughed.

Now, as if through a hole in the ceiling, I can see myself, small for my age, too skinny, thoroughly embarrassed. By now I had seen that none of my friends were there, and among the several men who had come in to loaf until bedtime I was the one boy. I was sorry I had come in, but I was too embarrassed to leave. If some of the women had been there it would have been better, for they would have been openly kind to a small boy, and being there among the men had made me aware again that I was a small boy. The men would not have been impressed to know that I had come alone by bus from Hargrave to Port

William. The women would have been there if it had been Saturday night, for on Saturdays whole families came to town to shop and visit. Weeknights you would find only the men, and only certain men, loafing about in the places of business and spending usually not enough money to pay the proprietors to keep a fire going and the lights on.

The conversation that these loafers kept going, night after night, was Port William's sole indigenous public institution. By it, the manhood at least of the town reminded itself of itself, preserved its history to the extent that it was preserved, entertained and comforted itself, and in some measure even governed itself. And though I could not have been aware of it then, there was kindness in it too, inadvertent as it may have been. For Port William always had its fair allotment of widowers and aging bachelors, lonely men who used these nighttime gatherings to fend off between darkfall and bedtime the thoughts that come to the lonely and are hard to suffer alone.

This kindness, however, lived below or beyond the masculine hardness and even the sometimes cruelty of laughter at somebody else's discomfort, or the ironies of Milton Burgess's mercantile manners, which for a moment or two had kept me paralyzed in my shyness. But then the bunch began to clarify itself and sort itself into individual people, most of whom I knew.

Before I came in, Mr. Athey Keith had been talking to Mr. Burgess, holding a paper bag of something and ready to leave. Mr. Keith did not loaf. He spoke to me and shook my hand—he was a friend of my grandfathers' and my father's—and this seemed to undo Mr. Burgess's officious silliness. Mr. Keith said, "How are you, young man?" thus, it seemed, both paying his respects to my family and telling me what he expected of me. He then went straight out the door, giving exactly as much heed to the loafers as if they had not been there at all.

Gathered in the back of the room to talk around the stove, seated on an assortment of chairs, crates, and kegs, were, among others, Grover Gibbs, Maze Tickburn, drunk, Fee Berlew, unusually sober, and, the youngest of them, Troy Chatham, who was Mr. Keith's son-in-law. It was Troy who had laughed. Jayber Crow, the barber, was leaning against a rank of shelved canned goods, his hands in his pockets, mainly listening as usual. Jayber was always good to me, as he was to everybody, and I went and stood beside him as I would have gone to shelter in a storm. He looked down at me and smiled, gave me two pats on the shoulder, and said, "How you doing, Andy?"

Grover Gibbs was sitting by Jayber on a nail keg. He stuck his big fist out at me and said, "Calf's head. Hit her a good one."

I had been onto that since I was about five. It would have been like hitting an anvil, and the harder you hit the worse it would hurt.

And so I just slapped his fist with my open hand. He jerked his fist back, rubbing it, and said in falsetto, "Oh! You hurt me, boy." The laughter that came from everybody then was friendly, and so I was all right.

Maze Tickburn was sitting in a rocking chair behind the stove, holding forth. He seemed to be in a fashion the host of the gathering, and certainly its chief entertainer. Maze was Port William's stonemason, its digger and waller-up of cisterns and wells, its builder of foundations and cellars. He lived with his

wife, India, on a scrap of hillside, two acres maybe, below the
road just after it started down the hill toward Dawes Landing
and eventually Hargrave. On their perch above the river valley,
Maze and India had a small house, a smaller barn, a pen for the
hog that ate their scraps, and the cistern, dug and walled and
plastered by Maze, that caught the rainwater from their roof.
On their stony slope they raised a garden and a little patch of
tobacco, but lived mostly on Maze's daily wage of perhaps two
dollars.

When he had steady work, Maze was a sober man. When he
didn't, usually in winter when the ground was too wet or too
hard-frozen to dig, idleness and the long nights would wear on
his nerves, and then he would drink and spend a good deal of
time in town. He especially endeared himself to his fellow loafers at these times because, when drunk, he sang whatever he
said. He made the music of his words principally by drawing out
certain sounds until their gravity was fully disclosed:

> Ohhhh, there's nothing so to warrrrm
> The heart like a droooop of whiskey
> On a coooold day.

Or he would brag:

> Ohhhh, I am the beeeest stone waaaaller
> What they iiiis in Porrrrt William
> On account of I aaaam the oooonliest one.
> But a feeeew moooore years
> And I'm a loooong time gone,
> And wheeeen I'm goooone
> They woooon't be noooone.

At such times Maze's thoughts dwelt upon mortality, and he would sing of Petey Tacker, the Hargrave undertaker:

Ollll' Petey Tacker, heeee's the boy
Aaaalways shoooore of a job,
Laaaast feller we'll eeeever meet.
And wheeeen I meet him
I'll doooone be done.
I'll be a loooong time gone.

I don't know if I'm remembering now from that night in 1943, or just remembering. Maze was a principal character in Port William, one of its stars, you might say, for a good many years after that, and he was remembered for a good many years more, is *still* remembered by a few who cherish such memories. If all the stories of Maze and their related songs had been remembered, they would make a sort of happenstance opera of Port William. For instance:

One day Mrs. Preston, wife of Brother Preston the young preacher, was driving home from Hargrave. She came around a curve and there was Maze wobbling in his derelict truck from one side of the road to the other. Mrs. Preston very considerately applied the brakes, and so she hit him just hard enough to pop him out and send him flying into a big briar patch. Maze took the shock limberly enough, and so sustained no serious injuries but only a multitude of scratches. When he landed he just sat there with his back against a stump, bleeding profusely from his head, face, neck, shoulders, arms, hands, and perhaps other parts.

Mrs. Preston crept on hands and knees through the tunnel Maze had bored going in, and when she saw him she sang a tremulous little aria of her own:

> Ohhhh, Mr. Tickburn!
> Are you allll riiiight?
> Can I heeeelp you?

And Maze sang back:

> Ohhhh, Mizriz Piston,
> Caaaall Petey Tacker,
> Gaaaather dog fennel,
> And siiiing "Blue Eyes."
> I'm a loooong time gone.

I do remember that on that night in Burgess's store Maze presently sang:

> Ooool' Milton Burgess,
> Most honestest maaaan ever lived!
> Buy twoooo pound of bloney,
> Get oooone pound and a haaaalf
> And haaaalf a pound of thuuuumb.
> Sellll you a load of coallll
> Eighteen huuuunderd to the toooon.

Milton Burgess, I think, was not a humorless man. If he was not highly entertained all his life, he missed a wonderful opportunity. But he understood too that he had his part to play in the ongoing drama. He responded in recitative: "Get him out of here!"

"I'm a loooong time gone," sang Maze over his shoulder as he helped himself to the door and out into the dark.

And perhaps I knew even then that Maze would make his way along the road to where the path to his house branched off and went steeply down the slope. And there he would stop, afraid to go farther alone, and sing that evening's closing song:

> Ohhhhhh, Indy!
> Ohhhhhh, Indy!
> Come get ollll' Maze!
> Ollll' somabitch
> Is druuuunk agin!

And India would come up the path to help him home.

❦

When Maze had gone and the conversation had resumed, I began to feel again the way I had felt that morning in the stripping room. I felt it was a good place in which I did not belong. Not yet. I was nine years old, going on ten, with the ambition of growing up to be a man good at work. I had even begun to learn to be such a man, as I can see now, but I was a long time and many difficulties short of my aim. Though I didn't want to know it, I knew that nobody could mistake me for anything but what I was: a small boy unaccomplished at much of anything except causing trouble.

I said, "What time is it, Jayber?"

He looked at his watch. "Quarter after seven."

"Well," I said, "I got to go."

As I went to the door, Mr. Burgess said, "Goodnight, Mr. Catlett. Call again, *please*."

Some of the older boys at school sometimes said to one another, "Kiss my ass." That expression came to my mind then and I recognized its excellence. But I was too near the door by then to say anything, even assuming I would have dared to say anything. If Granny heard I had told Mr. Burgess to kiss my ass, she would have used all the soap in Port William to wash out my mouth.

Outside it was cold and just about perfectly black. It had clouded up again, not a star in the whole sky. I stood still a minute, just to feel the relief of being out of the store and out of sight. Lighted windows here and there shone through the dark without brightening it.

Granny had turned on the porch light for me. I headed for that, and was soon back again where everybody was glad to see me. They were all sitting in the living room, talking. I hung up my wraps on the hall tree and went in and sat on the sofa between Hannah and Aunt Lizzie. Uncle Ernest had gone up to his room over the kitchen. All the rest were there.

They were talking about Uncle Virgil. They all had written to him at Christmas, had sent him presents, and by then had received his letters in reply. Now they were repeating what he had said. Since he had gone, an insistent dread had dwelt in that house, never spoken of, not at least in my hearing. I did not think of it all the time, but when I did think of it, there it would be. Perhaps it never departed from Hannah and my grandparents. I think of them now, of Hannah then scarcely more than a girl, hardly more conversant with the death she dreaded than I was, and of my grandparents, to whom that death when it came would be one of a series to which they knew their own belonged. It was as though their talk of Uncle Virgil that night, talk that was humorous and bright and hopeful, was yet overlaid by a shadow; and my memory of it, as I look back with knowledge, is overlaid by grief.

But the talk then drifted on from Uncle Virgil to other things, to common memories, old stories told again, and to the ever-returning questions of history and kinship: long discussions, sometimes contentious, beginning "Whatever happened to their daughter?" or "Who did he marry?" or "Who was she before she married?" And again I wish I had listened.

My own mind too drifted away from the subject of Uncle Virgil, but it followed its own course of thought. For me, in addition to its present foreboding, that house contained my mother's memories of her girlhood and growing up, which I had so sharply imagined as to make them almost my own: stories of walking down to the river to swim; of skating parties at Grover's Pond; of how Aunt Cass had let her fall onto the stove top, blistering the palms of her hands; of how she rode on her pony out the Coulter lane at dusk and was sent flying home by the moaning of pigeons in a barn; of putting on a circus in which so many Port Williamites performed that hardly enough were left for an audience.

The sense of a longer, older history that came to me in my ancestral houses came mostly from my grandmothers, both of whom had lived in the early years of their marriages with their mothers-in-law, my grandfathers' mothers. Both of my grandmothers, despite their remarkable differences of character, never complained of that state of things, but they seemed to have done a great deal of listening. Their own memories included the memories of the older women, and they spoke familiarly of lifetimes not their own. And so in both houses I knew, before I knew what to think of it, a history that seemed to me ancient and that included much sorrow: memories of hard births, hard work, epidemics, deaths of children, debt and worry. And always back there in the mists of time, hardly imaginable and yet immediate as an odor, was the Civil War and the violence and personal vengeances, tawdry and deadly, that it had perpetrated in the little towns and farm neighborhoods of our part of the country.

❧

In one of the corners of that room were glass-fronted shelves of books. Some of them still would be considered good books: books by Scott and Dickens and Hawthorne and Mark Twain. They had belonged to Granddaddy's mother, and in a good many of them her name was written on the flyleaf in a pretty hand: "Nancy Beechum Feltner." There were some books in those cases that I knew Ma Feltner had read to my mother when she was a girl. I had not read any of those books yet, though I imagined that eventually I would. But one of them especially attracted me. This was an early edition of *The Adventures of*

Huckleberry Finn with the illustrations of E. W. Kemble. It was the copy I would read in another year or two, and I have it yet, the pages now so fragile they will hardly bear touching. But in those days, in 1943, I was taking it out only to look at the pictures. I thought of going to get it, and then I thought of *The Boy's King Arthur* in which would be the sound of my mother's voice. I loved the sound of her voice reading, I think, above all the other sounds I knew. I rested in it. Among my most estimable experiences was that of being sick in the wintertime, free from school, alone at home with my mother. Those days brought precious exceptions and variances. I could spend the day downstairs in my parents' bed. I could have poached eggs and toast and tea. And my mother would read to me: *The Swiss Family Robinson, Treasure Island, Little Men,* the stories of Robin Hood and Little John and Friar Tuck and Much the Miller's Son, *A Christmas Carol.* In this house that had once been hers I felt both separated from her and close to the thought of her.

I got the book out of my suitcase in the hall and went back to my place on the sofa. I turned to the illustration that I liked maybe best of any, a picture of Sir Launcelot gone mad in the woods after Queen Guenever had so mistakenly told him to stay out of her sight. Except for Sir Launcelot's eyes, which were rather too bugged-out with his madness, it is an inviting picture: a wilderness of old trees and big rocks and a little falling stream. And on the facing page I read, hearing my mother's voice quietly bespeaking the strangeness and wonderfulness of the words as she pronounced them:

> *And now leave we a little of Sir Ector and Sir Percival, and*
> *speak we of Sir Launcelot, that suffered and endured many sharp*

showers, which ever ran wild wood, from place to place, and lived by fruit and such as he could get, and drank water, two years; and other clothing had he but little, save his shirt and his breeches.

It didn't sound like such a bad life. Much as I admired Sir Launcelot, I was disappointed in him for allowing himself to be driven crazy by Queen Guenever. If she had forbidden me to come into her sight, I would not have minded much.

It pleased me thoroughly to know that back in those old days the word for crazy was "wood." But this was going to get me in trouble in a few weeks, when we fourth graders started learning about synonyms. Our teacher, Miss Heartsease, sent a number of us to the blackboard to write down a word, any word, and a synonym. I wrote "crazy — wood." This was my first performance as a cutting-edge scholar, and I am sure I was too obviously proud of it. Maybe I expected to be asked to address the class on the subject of Arthurian synonyms. But Miss Heartsease, who no doubt had been denied the benefits of *The Boys' King Arthur,* was not impressed. She thought I was merely striking another blow for the emancipation of fourth graders, and she sent me back to my seat in disgrace. This gave so much pleasure to my classmates that they had to be called to order, which gave me even more pleasure than the rarity of my synonym. Thus, though it was not in the curriculum, I was learning at an early age one of the laws of compensation: cutting-edge scholarship, even when unappreciated, is effective as entertainment.

I turned in the book past the place where my mother had stopped reading to me, and a wonderful thing happened.

The sound of my mother's voice reading that strange English continued in my mind, and I realized that I was reading it for myself, but in her voice. I read how Sir Tristram went mad for love of the queen, la Belle Isolda, so that she did not recognize him:

> But ever she said unto Dame Bragwaine, "Me seemeth I should have seen him heretofore in many places."
>
> But as soon as Sir Tristram saw her he knew her well enough, and then he turned away his visage and wept. Then the queen had always a little brachet with her, that Sir Tristram gave her the first time that ever she came into Cornwall . . . And anon as this little brachet felt a savor of Sir Tristram, she leaped upon him, and licked his learis and his ears, and then she whined and quested, and she smelled at his feet and at his hands, and on all parts of his body that she might come to.

So then I knew what a brachet was. But Sir Tristram was the second knight I had read about who had gone mad for love of a woman. This seemed to me to be happening too often, even if the women were queens. I didn't think I would ever fall in love with an actual queen, but it did trouble me to wonder if ever I would be driven out of my mind by love for a woman. Because I would soon write my age in two numerals, I was afraid something like that might happen to me pretty soon. But by now life has pretty much had its way with me, and I can say with relief that I have never gone mad for love. Not completely.

It was becoming clear to me that this book needed to have an end, and I turned a lot farther over, and read a little about the death of King Arthur, how the King when he was dying sent Sir Bedivere to throw his beautiful sword Excalibur into the water, and how Sir Bedivere disobeyed twice but finally obeyed:

> *Then Sir Bedivere departed, and went to the sword, and lightly took it up, and went to the water's side; and there he bound the girdle about the hilts, and then he threw the sword into the water as far as he might; and there came an arm and an hand above the water, and met it and caught it, and so shook it thrice and brandished.*
>
> *And then the hand vanished away with the sword in the water.*

I could just *see* that, and what I saw was a knight in beautiful armor walking down through the woods to the rockbar at the mouth of Coulter Branch on our own river. He carried reverently in both hands a beautiful sword. He went out to the very edge of the rockbar and threw the sword as far as he could into the river, and just as I was ready for the splash it was going to make, a hand rose up out of the water and caught it!

"I think I see a sleepy boy," Granny said, and I sat up straight to try not to look sleepy.

"Well, Granny," Granddaddy said, looking serious, "we haven't got a bed for him. I reckon we'll have to hang him on a nail."

He said that every time I came to spend the night, and I laughed. I said, "Where's the nail?"

But Granny, who was not always sure herself when Granddaddy was teasing, said, "Granddaddy's teasing you." She got up. "You just come with Granny. Nobody's going to have to hang on a nail around here. Tell everybody goodnight."

That meant I got to let Hannah kiss me again. I made the rounds to get and give my goodnight hugs:

"Goodnight, Auntie. Goodnight, Granddaddy. Goodnight, Aunt Lizzie. Goodnight, Hannah."

And Hannah did give me another excellent kiss on the cheek.

❧

I picked up my grip and my book, and Granny and I went up the stairs. We went to the bedroom in the back of the house that had been Ma Feltner's room in her last years and then my mother's when she was growing up. It was a small, comfortable room on the south side. The sun shone in through the window in the winter, making a warm print of light on the rug, and often in the summer a breeze would sway the curtains as it blew in through the shade of the old maples in the yard.

Granny turned back the bed for me and plumped the pillow and turned on the lamp on the nightstand. There was a little radio on the nightstand.

"You can listen to the radio if you want to," Granny said, "but don't turn it up loud."

She knew I would like to listen awhile, for Henry and I didn't have a radio in our room at home.

She said, "Now, you brought your pajamas?"

"Yes, mam."

"And you've got your toothbrush?"

"Yes, mam."

"Well, take a bath and brush your teeth. I know I can depend on you to do that."

I said, "Yes, mam, you can." I had been afraid she might wash my ears herself, just to make sure. She was a gentle, truly good woman whose chief pleasure was in the happiness of other people, but when she went at one of your ears it felt like her finger was going to bore clean through your head and come out the other side.

"Don't be too long," she said. "Other people will be wanting to get in there. And don't use too much water. Now come here and kiss your granny goodnight."

I gave her a hug and a kiss and she left me. Feeling on my own again and responsible, I got my pajamas and my toothbrush out of my grip and went into the bathroom. I ran some water, but not too much, into the tub, and proceeded in pretty much of a hurry through all the before-bed requirements. I even did a thorough job on my ears, in them and behind them, and I brushed my teeth.

When I was in bed and the lovely feeling of that house and my welcome in it had come over me, I turned the radio on just loud enough to hear and turned out the light.

The radio brought the great world into that dark small room. It was the next-to-last night of the year, and the people on the radio were talking on the theme of time, of the old year that was passing away and the new year that was about to begin. The year of 1943, they said, had been a bloody and a murderous one. Many people had died, many had been hurt. Time and history had passed heavily over our poor world and had left it wounded and grieving. And what of the next year, 1944? Well, we would hope and pray for peace. We would hope and pray that our loved ones would come safely home. That would be our offering to that new year: a prayer for peace. Let the killing stop. Let the blood and the tears cease to flow. Let Uncle Virgil come home and never again have to go away.

The actual year of 1944 would be as bloody, in fact, as the one before and the one after. And in that year, shortly before my tenth birthday, Uncle Andrew, my father's brother, would be shot and killed, not overseas in the war but here at home. And his began a series of deaths and losses that in the coming years would change the world as I had known it, and would change me: Dick Watson's, Uncle Virgil's, Uncle Ernest's, Grandpa's. The losses and griefs that are passing always over the world would come to us, breaking like waves upon the family houses. After Dick's death Aunt Sarah Jane moved to Louisville, never to be heard from again. In a few more years the Brightleafs would be gone. At the Feltner place, Joe Banion would die, and Nettie and Aunt Fanny would move away, like Aunt Sarah Jane, to be near relatives who had gone to the city. And so that year of 1943 was in a sense my last year of innocence, of the illusion of permanence and peace. I was about to enter the time that is told by change, by death and loss, by the absence of the past and its members. By now, of all the people I have been remembering from those days in Port William, I alone am still alive. I am, as Maze Tickburn used to say, the onliest one.

Lying in bed that night, in the midst of my journey alone to my home places, still free of all that was to come, I felt even so the current of time flowing over me and over the house and through all the dark night outside. For a longish while, before sleep finally overtook my thoughts, I would have given a lot to see my mother.

※

Time is told by death, who doubts it? But time is always halved—for all we know, it is halved—by the eye blink, the synapse, the immeasurable moment of the present. Time is only the past and maybe the future; the present moment, dividing and connecting them, is eternal. The time of the past is there, somewhat, but only somewhat, to be remembered and examined. We believe that the future is there too, for it keeps arriving, though we know nothing about it. But try to stop the present for your patient scrutiny, or to measure its length with your most advanced chronometer. It exists, so far as I can tell, only as a leak in time, through which, if we are quiet enough, eternity falls upon us and makes its claim. And here I am, an old man, traveling as a child among the dead.

We measure time by its deaths, yes, and by its births. For time is told also by life. As some depart, others come. The hand opened in farewell remains open in welcome. I, who once had grandparents and parents, now have children and grandchildren. Like the flowing river that is yet always present, time that is always going is always coming. And time that is told by death and birth is held and redeemed by love, which is always present. Time, then, is told by love's losses, and by the coming of love, and by love continuing in gratitude for what is lost. It is folded and enfolded and unfolded forever and ever, the love by which the dead are alive and the unborn welcomed into the womb. The great question for the old and the dying, I think, is not if they have loved and been loved enough, but if they have been grateful enough for love received and given, however much. No one who has gratitude is the onliest one. Let us pray to be grateful to the last.

🌱

I woke to the sound of Granny's rapping on a pipe in the kitchen to tell Uncle Ernest in the room above that breakfast would be ready before long. She did that every morning, and it was a good sort of telegraph, for the plumbing carried her signal all over the house. It was still dark. Had Granny turned off the radio after I went to sleep? It was silent, and I didn't remember turning it off. I switched on the light and dressed and ran down to the kitchen.

Though the daylight would not come for a while yet, the night was finished. Auntie and Aunt Lizzie were stirring in their room, Uncle Ernest in his, Hannah in hers. Granddaddy had made his and Granny's bed and gone to the barn. Granny and Nettie Banion were busy in the kitchen, which was full of the smells of coffee and frying bacon.

"*Here* he is," Granny said when I came into the kitchen. "Hungry too, I expect."

And Nettie turned away from the stove and said, "Good morning to you, Andy Catlett."

I said, "Hello, Nettie. How're you?"

She said, "Just fine!"

And Granny said, "Did you wash? You didn't. Go do it."

I went and washed my hands and face and even wet my hair and combed it.

Granddaddy soon came in with the milk and went to wash up. And then it wasn't long until we all were there. All of us sat down, except for Granny and Nettie, who were putting the food on the table. And then Granny sat down, leaving Nettie to pour coffee for the grownups and milk for me, and to see that everybody had enough of everything. There were eggs and bacon and hot biscuits and two kinds of jam. And of course there was no end of talk, for the night seemed to have filled everybody's mind with new subjects.

When we had finished, Granny and Hannah cleaned the table and started washing the dishes. Nettie fixed breakfast for herself and Joe, and set their places at the table. Joe came in from the barn, and the two of them sat down to eat. I sat on at the table with Nettie and Joe while they ate, for I was glad to see them.

Whereas the hired help out at my Catlett grandparents' came and went, the Banions had worked for the Feltners since way back. I am not quite up to explaining this. Whether or not the Banions had once been slaves of the Feltners, I don't know. That is something else I should have asked before it was too late. I know only that the two families had been together at least since the time of Ma and Pa Feltner, the time of Smoke and Cass, who were Joe's grandparents, and who, if they were not on the place during slavery, had come soon after. And the two families had belonged there together ever since.

Of the two of us, I think my brother Henry was Joe's favorite. When our whole family would come to visit, Joe's biggest greeting would be to Henry. He would begin to laugh just at the sight of Henry, who had the look of being ready to "put the cat in the churn," as Uncle Jack Beechum said.

"*Look* out, Henry!" Joe would say and put up his fists, and he and Henry would spar a round while everybody laughed.

But Joe was good to me too. Now that I was getting bigger, he would sometimes let me follow him into the woods. He was a squirrel hunter, and on those jaunts he would be much stricter with me than Dick Watson ever was. More than anybody, Joe Banion taught me how to be quiet, and how to look until I saw. When he would turn on me with a peremptory motion of his hand and say "Hersh!" I would hush in mid-word without the further commotion even of shutting my mouth. And when, creeping along silently and seeing, I believed, all there was to see, he would turn to me—"All right. Where's he at?"—I would feel under tremendous pressure to pick out the squirrel in his stillness among all the deceptions of leaves and shadows.

Seeing Joe had put hunting on my mind and started me into the very jabber from which, in the woods, he would have required me to "hersh." About as much as I wanted a mule of my own, and much more than I wanted a BB gun, I wanted to have my own .22 rifle. I knew that for a boy of nine going on ten, in my family, this was a wish without hope, but I started telling Joe Banion how careful I would be with my rifle, if I had one. Partly, this was for Granny to overhear and tell my mother.

Joe knew what I was up to, and to egg me on he obliged me by agreeing with me. "Oh, yes!" he said. "Oh, I imagine!"

✤

Joe, who had been up and busy a long time, made short work of a large breakfast, saving his coffee until last to prolong his leisure. With a grace surprising in hands so work-stiffened, he saucered the coffee, blew upon it, and supped it up in savorous whiffs.

And then, the day having established its pattern and its claim upon him, he got up and put on his cap and jacket and gloves. He hunched his shoulders in anticipation of the cold wind. "Airish out," he said. He complimented the breakfast, "Mighty fine," and went out.

Daylight had come strong enough now to see out the windows even with the light on in the kitchen. From where I sat at the table, I could look out across the ridges and the wooded hollows on our side of the river and on to the ridgetops and the tiny barns and houses on the far side. The limbs of the trees in the yard were swaying in the wind. After the one sunny day, it was cloudy again, and when Joe and Granddaddy had opened the back door, I had felt the cold. Every time that door had opened and shut again the warmth of the house had felt better.

I went upstairs and made my bed without waiting for Granny to tell me, in the process remembering that I had not made my bed out at Grandma's. I had not given it a thought since I had got out of it the morning before. And that made me remember to brush my teeth without being told. Out the window of my room I could see the church and the post office and the hotel and some of the storefronts of the town. Port William had been awake and about its business for a long time. Several men were already standing in a row, leaning against Jasper Lathrop's store, talking. One of Uncle Ernest's fictions for Henry and me, when we were little, was that the stores in Port William would fall down if several men didn't lean against them all the time. It still seemed strange and wonderful to me that the night could pass, so great an event of darkness, and there Port William would be again, just as it was before.

I went back down to the living room — the room that Granny always referred to from the kitchen as "in yonder"—and took Ma Feltner's old green edition of *Huckleberry Finn* out of the bookcase and sat down on the sofa. I looked at Ma Feltner's signature on the fly leaf and the date under it, "1886." I turned through it, looking for the pictures of the river, the greatest river, that bore in its currents the waters of every stream and river I knew. I loved the scenes of boats or rafts on the wide flatness of the water. I read the captions as I went along. And then I got to the one of a forest on the riverbank somewhere way down south, in which a tree in the foreground has its branches all hung with Spanish moss. My mother had explained to me about Spanish moss, and I had looked at the picture so much and thought so much about it that it had become a sort of dream to me. It looked so strange and far away that I still shivered when I looked at it.

I closed the book on that faraway place and sat still to let the familiar house take shape around me again. Presently the clock on the mantel chimed the quarter-hour. Of all the things I loved in that house, I loved that clock maybe the most, for the sound of it signaled the presence of everything else. It played in stately measure a quarter of its tune at a quarter past the hour, half at half past, three-quarters at a quarter till, and the whole again to announce the hour. That tune, when I ring it over in my mind now, calls back into presence the house as it was, all its rooms and furnishings, its sounds and smells.

At the sound of the clock that morning I got up and wandered about the house to see what people were doing. Using a little foreknowledge, I pretty soon found Hannah sitting by herself at a window in the dining room. She had made this her workplace, out of the way of the regular work of the household and yet near enough to keep her available to help when she was needed. She was doing needlepoint, making covers for the seats of chairs that would be in the house that she and Uncle Virgil were going to build and live in when the war would be over and he would come home. She came alone to this task for a little while every day, and I understood, as all the others did, that this was her enactment of her hope. It was a hope doomed to lie in all our minds like a ruined nest, but then it was a hope merely bright that lent its distinction to the love I felt for her.

She looked up and smiled when I came in and spread her work so I could see its nearly completed floral design.

"It's really pretty," I said, for it really was.

I sat down and she resumed her work. The window looked out toward the opening of the river valley and the uplands on the far side. Hannah had been born and raised over in that country.

"Can you see your old house from here?" I asked. I didn't think you could, but I wanted to hear her tell about her girlhood in her grandmother's decaying old house.

"No," she said, "you can't see it from here, but it's still over there."

"When you were a girl over there, did you ever think someday you'd be living over here?" I asked because the question seemed to require thinking about. I had begun to be surprised by the extent to which life consists of surprises. I didn't know but what it consisted mostly of surprises.

"Not an idea in this world," she said. "I didn't even know that 'over here' was over here."

"So all this is a surprise?"

"Yep. Every bit of it."

"Well, do you like it over here better than over there?"

"Some things over there I miss. My grandmother, I miss her. But there are a lot of things over here I like." She gave me a pat to let me know I was one of the things over here that she liked. "And some things over there I don't miss."

She spoke then of her stepmother, Ivy, and of her two mean stepbrothers, Ivy's boys Elvin and Allen.

Usually I was grateful for Elvin and Allen, who made me feel superior, for I was sure that I would never have been mean to Hannah if I had been her stepbrother. But her mention of their names that morning reminded me of a recent event that I had succeeded in forgetting entirely for the past two days and would just as soon have kept forgotten.

Just before school let out for Christmas, I had had a fight, an actual bodily fight, with a girl. I no longer remember the incidental details, but I am sure that I cannot have been innocent in this matter. I am in fact sure that I had given a grievous insult to my memorable classmate, Agnes Lee Lilly, but I did not know beforehand how grievous an insult it was, nor was I prepared for Agnes Lee's response.

We boys fought each other with some frequency in those days, during recess or after school, and I had done my share of this. But when boys fought boys, as I was about to learn from Agnes Lee, there were certain commonly respected limits. There were certain things we did not do to one another. For instance, we did not try to kill each other; we were not yet mature enough for that. But when Agnes Lee sought vengeance against me, she did so with the apparent intent to kill. She opened the proceedings without warning by hitting me on the head with her entire armload of schoolbooks. She then flung down the books and went at me with tooth and claw. She hit, bit, scratched, kicked, and pulled hair. I fought back, not because of any difference of opinion I may have had with her, but because I wished to stay alive.

Our teacher, Miss Heartsease, who had witnessed all this from her classroom window at a distance of about a hundred yards, raised the sash and cried out, "Stop that! Stop that! Stop this instant!"

I was glad enough to stop, even at the command of Miss Heartsease. And I was grateful to Agnes Lee for being similarly obedient.

When we had stopped, Miss Heartsease instructed Agnes Lee to go straight home and me to return to the classroom, where she kept me under arrest and under further instruction for a longish while. She deduced, from preceding evidence too freely supplied by me, that I was altogether at fault, having so far lowered myself as to strike a young lady.

She did not need to tell me never to do so again, for I had learned that lesson for myself; the next time I insulted a girl I would have a running start. But Miss Heartsease did tell me at length never to do so again. As she spoke, her eyes were moistly shining with righteous indignation and the satisfaction of fulfilled prophecy. She didn't allow me to open my mouth in my own defense, and the awfulness of her indictment was itself a punishment.

Well, may Heaven bless her corky old heart, for against my will and her intention she taught me valuable lessons — about, for example, the limits of self-defense.

At that time, however, I did not feel so charitable toward her. Her righteous vehemence and certainty had put me in much uncertainty, for I was fairly assured of my guilt and yet I did not feel guilty. I felt, in fact, somewhat more than adequately punished.

Even so, as I listened to Hannah's stories of those villains Elvin and Allen, I was fervently supposing that she hadn't heard about my recent dispute with Agnes Lee, and I was carefully keeping my mouth shut.

❧

Granddaddy had gone down into town after breakfast, I didn't know what for. But I knew he was on the bank board and was trusted, and people depended on him for things. When he got back to the house, he came on to the dining room door and looked in.

"Come on, son. Time to go to work."

I knew he wanted me to go with him, and I sort of wanted to, but I knew too that it was a bitter morning outside, and mostly I didn't want to go. The weather made it lovely to imagine a whole morning snug in the house, listening to the sounds of housekeeping and cooking and the women talking.

"Well," I said, "I think I'd rather just stay here."

I have reason to believe that he would not have accepted that reply from my mother or Uncle Virgil when they were young. But I was different. I was his grandson, more my parents' responsibility than his, and, after all, still a boy.

He just laughed a little to himself and said, "Well. All right." I heard him go through the house and out the back door.

But it was not long until Granny came in. She said in her gentle way, "Andy, your granddaddy has some work that he needs you to help him with," and I knew I had to go.

She had a promptitude of goodness that could be just fierce. She knew in an instant when I was dishonest or thoughtless or wrong. Much of my growing up, it seems to me now, was quietly required of me by her. She would correct me — "Listen to Granny. I expected something better from you" — and it would be as if in my mind a pawl had dropped into a notch; there was to be no going back.

I went and got my outdoor things, put them on, and went out the back door. It was cold, and to make things worse a few freezing raindrops were coming down in a slant along the raw wind. I walked through the chicken yard where a few of Granddaddy's old hens were standing around with their tails drooped, looking miserable. They looked like I felt. I was full of reluctance and embarrassment and shrunken in my clothes from the cold.

Where Granddaddy was I had no idea, for I had not asked. I went through the gate on the far end of the chicken yard and into the field behind the barn, listening all the time.

And then I heard Joe Banion speak in the driveway of the barn: "Come up." And he came out, standing on a hay wagon drawn by his team of mules, old Mary and old Jim. "Whoa-ho!" he said when he saw me. "I reckon you just as well get on."

"I reckon I just as well," I said, and I got on.

Joe drove up to the tobacco barn on the highest part of the ridge. When we came even with the front of the barn Joe stopped the team again. "They inside," he told me. I jumped down and he drove on.

I didn't know who "they" would be, but when I went through the front door, standing wide open to let in the light, I saw that they were Granddaddy and Burley Coulter.

The Coulters, Burley and his brother, Jarrat, had housed tobacco in that barn, but now they had emptied it. What Granddaddy and Burley were doing that morning was preparing the barn for the lambing that was due to begin in just a few days. Because they had used the barn, this was partly the Coulters' responsibility, and Burley had come to help. I was still feeling ashamed and a little odd because of my refusal, and so when I had stepped through the door I just stopped.

There was a large rick of baled alfalfa in one corner of the barn, put there to be handy to feed the lambing ewes. Granddaddy and Burley were building a low partition around it to keep the ewes from ruining it before they could eat it. Granddaddy was starting to nail up a board, and Burley was sorting through a stack of old lumber.

The first to notice me was Granddaddy. He said, "Hello, son."

And then Burley turned to look and said, "Well! If it ain't Andy!"

It was a moment not possible to forget. Tom Coulter, who not long ago had been killed in the fighting in Italy, was Burley's nephew. Part of the blood that had been shed in that bad year of 1943 had been Tom Coulter's. I had not seen Burley since the news of Tom's death had come. I didn't have grown-up manners, and I didn't know what to say. When Burley spoke to me, it was as if he was not just greeting or welcoming me, but receiving me into his tenderness for Tom. It put a lump in my throat. He came over, taking off his right glove, and shook my hand.

He said, "How you making it, old boy?"

I just nodded, afraid if I said "Fine" I would cry.

Granddaddy said, "Andy, pick up the other end of this board, honey."

I picked it up and held it while he nailed his end. And then he came over and nailed my end. We did the same with the next board. And so I was helping. All through the morning they kept finding ways for me to help. They let me belong there at work with them. They kept me busy. And I experienced a beautiful change that was still new to me then but is old and familiar now. I went from reluctance and dread to interest in what we were doing, and then to pleasure in it. I got warm.

We finished the barrier around the hay rick. We picked up everything that was out of place or in the way. We made the barn neat. Joe returned with a load of straw from the straw stack. And then we bedded the barn, carrying forkloads of straw from the wagon and shaking it out level and deep over the whole floor, replacing the old fragrance of tobacco with the new fragrance of clean straw. Granddaddy had some long panels that would be used, as soon as needed, to portion the barn between the ewes with lambs and those still to lamb. We repaired the panels and propped them against the walls where they would be handy. We unstacked the mangers and lined them up in a row down the center of the driveway. Along one wall we set up the four-by-four-foot lambing pens where the ewes with new lambs would be confined and watched over until the lambs were well-started and strong—"the maternity ward," Granddaddy called it.

The men were letting me help sometimes even when I could see I was slowing them down. We transformed the barn from a tobacco barn recalling last summer's crop to a sheep barn expecting next year's lambs. In our work we could feel the new year coming, the days lengthening, the time of birth and growth returning, and this seemed to bring a happiness to everybody, in spite of the war and people's griefs and fears. The last thing we did was clean up the stripping room. It would be a sort of hospital, where Granddaddy, when he would be watching in the cold nights, could build a fire and help with a difficult birth, or pen a ewe with weak lambs until the lambs had sucked and were well dried, or keep orphan lambs until they got a good start.

When we were done at last, Granddaddy looked at his watch and then at me. "Well," he said, "could you eat a little something?"

The whole morning had gone by already, and I had not

thought of hunger, but now when I thought of it I was hungry. I said, "I could eat a *lot* of something."

We laughed, and Burley said, "His belly thinks his throat's been cut."

"Burley," Granddaddy said, "won't you come have a bite of dinner with us?"

And Burley said, "Naw, Mat. Thank you. I left some dinner on the stove at home. I better go see about it."

Joe took the team and wagon back to the feed barn then, and I went with Granddaddy to drive Burley out to his house.

By the time we got back and washed, everybody was in the kitchen. Nettie was finishing up at the stove and Granny and Hannah were putting the food on the table. The smell of it seemed fairly to hollow me out inside. We had sausage and gravy and mashed potatoes, just like at Grandma's. Granny's sausage was seasoned differently but was just as good. And we had, besides, hominy and creamed butter beans and, instead of biscuits, hoecake—one already on the table, sliced, another on the griddle—a pitcher of fresh milk, coffee for the grown-ups, and again all the Christmas desserts, and again, for me, ice cream.

"Save room," Granny said again.

And I said, "I'm going to have plenty of room."

I had more room even than I thought.

Hannah said, "Do you think he'll leave us anything to eat tomorrow?"

"I don't know," Granddaddy said. "We may have to skip a day or two."

"Granddaddy," I said, "what are we going to do this after-noon?"

"Oh, not much," Granddaddy said. "We've got things in pretty good shape."

When we were finished, Joe came in, and he and Nettie sat down to their dinner. I lost track of Granddaddy. He had gone, I imagine, to look at his ewes, as he had done the first thing that morning and would again before dark.

"Andy," Granny said, rewarding me now, "your book is still in yonder on the sofa. Why don't you go in there a while?"

I felt wonderfully at peace. Except for that little slipup in the morning, I had been good. I seemed to have got back safely within the approval of everybody. In fact, I had been pretty good going on three days. School seemed hardly rememberable. The difficulty of being good at home and at school both at once seemed far away.

I picked up the old copy of *Huckleberry Finn* and lay down on the sofa. And then I truly fell under the influence of peace and warmth and my morning's work and a full stomach. I was asleep before I could open the book.

❧

I slept soundly and long, dreamlessly except I dreamed I was there asleep. And then my eyes opened. That, it seemed, was what woke me. Otherwise, I did not move. I lay there a long time without moving. My body was a still, comfortable place where I lay asleep. The house too was still. I could hear the quiet in every one of its rooms. It was breathing in a sort of waking sleep, like mine.

I could not move until the quiet ended. And then the clock on the mantel chimed the half-hour. The quiet returned, as if at the final "dong" time had stopped.

I got up. Walking so as not to make a sound, I went back to the kitchen. Granny was sitting by one of the windows with her sewing basket and button box and a heap of Granddaddy's and Uncle Ernest's work shirts beside her on the table. She was patching torn places and replacing buttons, making the shirts last. She too was not making a sound. She was under the spell of her own quietness in the quiet house, and was enjoying being alone.

When I came in, she looked up and smiled. "Well, old sleepy-head, are you awake?"

I came over to stand beside her where I could watch her. "I'm awake," I said. We were talking quietly so that the greater quiet of the house and the afternoon stayed intact around us. "Where is everybody?"

"Auntie and Aunt Lizzie have gone visiting. Hannah took them in the car."

I stood and watched her for a while. She was putting on a patch, stabbing the needle in, helping it with her thimble, and drawing it out, all in one fluent motion that she repeated again and again rapidly. I knew her mastery at her work, for in all my own attempts at sewing my motions were awkward and slow, my stitches unlike and irregular.

"I don't know how you do that," I said.

"I don't either," she said. "I forgot how to do this a long time ago. I just do it."

The patch, finished, looked prettier to me than the cloth that was unpatched. She whipped in a knot and cut the thread, and then she held up the shirt and looked it over.

I said, "Where's Granddaddy?"

"I don't know," she said. She was getting ready to rethread her needle. "But if I wanted to find him, I know where I'd go look."

"Where?"

"Well, you know that little room in Jasper's store that he used for an office?"

"Yes, mam."

"That's where I'd look."

When I was out of the house, standing on the walk in front, the quiet seemed still to be unbroken. I had come out of a smaller quiet into the larger one that contained it. The wind had laid. Every tree was standing still. The overcast had thinned, and under it the light had brightened. Down in town the road was empty. There was not a soul in sight. The fronts of all the buildings looked permanently shut.

In the other direction, out toward the river valley, the country was as quiet, as still, as the town. One trance held everything. Under the gray sky, the light was strong. Every detail, every fencepost and tree, every door and window in every building, was steady and clear, luminous, as if the things of the earth had absorbed the light of the sky. On the farthest ridge, this side of the valley, I could see Uncle Virgil's cattle lying down. The whole country seemed to be meditating on itself, as if consciously submitted to whatever was to come. I remembered it was New Year's Eve. It was only another day, though already a little longer than yesterday, but I felt as if a great page was about to turn.

Suspended in that rapt light at the edge of time, so that my footfalls made no sound, I crossed the road and went down to Jasper Lathrop's store. In spite of Granny's assurance, I was a little surprised when the latch gave and the door opened. I went in and shut the door as carefully as I had opened it.

And then I had to stop and look. I had not been in there since Jasper got his call and went off to the army. I had not, I think, even looked in the windows. I remembered it fully stocked with groceries and hardware, all the varied merchandise of a general store in those days, and occupied by shoppers and loafers and Jasper himself. Now it was empty. Completely empty. Every shelf and bin and counter was as bare of goods as Mother Hubbard's cupboard. The store contained only its share of the surrounding stillness, and the light starkly shaped and shadowed by the deserted furnishings.

From the back, presently, came the sound of a voice saying something too quietly for me to understand. The voice, like Granny's and mine a while ago in the kitchen, spoke as if under a spell. After it spoke the quiet remained.

With the same strict observance I walked back one of the aisles of the large room toward the smaller room in the back.

I heard another voice and then another one, quiet as before.

I felt I should knock and I did, lightly.

"Come in," one of the voices said, only a little louder. The door was not even latched. I pushed and it opened.

They were sitting around Jasper's meat block, playing rummy: Granddaddy, Frank Lathrop who was Jasper's father, Grover Gibbs, Burley Coulter, Jayber Crow. When I opened the door they greeted me with nods, smiles, lifted hands.

"Come in, Andy," Jayber said.

There were empty chairs here and there, and so evidently the game sometimes had onlookers or more players. I stepped in, shut the door, and sat down in the nearest chair. The quiet went on. The players were concentrating on their game and took no more notice of me.

They had a good coal fire going in the stove, and the room was warm. It was full of tobacco smoke, which hazed the cold light flowing in from the two westward windows. At the end of the room opposite the stove was a roll-top desk with its top shut. Above the desk, lined up, were several boxes with labels, and a radio, turned on but hardly audible. Tacked to the wall by the door was a large sheet of brown paper with maybe a dozen names written across the top and under each name a column of figures. Years later, when I had grown old enough to wonder and to ask, Jayber told me that they never declared a winner, never totaled the scores, but just let the numbers accumulate on that brown sheet until the war ended, when they ceased to pay it any mind. Jayber guessed that when Jasper came home and re-started his business he must have wadded up the scores and burnt them in the stove.

Out the windows the lot behind the store was scrawled over with dead weed stalks. More or less in the middle of it was a bunch of old wooden crates, boxes, baskets, and such, all cluttered together in a pile. Drawing a straight edge to that zone of neglect was a woven wire fence, and beyond that a large pasture that rose gently up to a barn on the horizon. A flock of sheep were lying at rest far up the slope on the dormant grass.

It was a comfortable place. I made myself at home. The card-players played on, intent upon their game, saying almost nothing. Only now and again somebody would mutter under the silence, "Well, I was wondering who had that ace" or "I can give that trey a good home." I watched not just them but everything. I was as wide awake as when I had drunk that coffee two days ago, except now I was quiet. I sat without moving.

The next evening Granddaddy would go with me to catch the bus on its daily trip to Hargrave, and I would complete my trip, alone as I had started, back to our house in the new year. It was going to be a year that would teach me something about loss that I had not learned in all the years before: It could happen to me. But there in that little room at the end of the old year, I was already learning something that I have never stopped learning and will never learn completely.

As I watched, it came to me that they were waiting: Grand-daddy and Frank Lathrop, each with a son in the army; Grover Gibbs, whose son, Billy, was in the air force; Burley Coulter, whose nephews, Tom and Nathan, had gone off to the army, and who now could hope that Nathan only might return; Jayber Crow, whose calling seems to have been to wait with the others. They were suffering and enduring and waiting, waiting together, joined in their unending game, submitted as the countryside around them was submitted. We had come into the silence that is deeper than any other—the silence of what is yet to come, the silence of one who is waiting for what is yet to come.

And now, as often before, I am reminded how grateful I am to have been there, in that time, with these I have remembered. I was there with them; they remain here with me. For in that little while Port William sank into me, becoming one with the matter and light, and the darkness, of my mind, never again to be far from my thoughts, no matter where I went or what I did.

Acknowledgments

Harland Hubbard said he saw no point in niggling over his work, and for himself I think he was right. But right or wrong for myself, I am a niggler. My work seems to become presentable finally because of many changes. Some of the changes are large; but most are small. This is because of the people who have helped me. I read my longhand draft of this book to Tanya Berry, who then made the first typescript. Later David and Tanya Charlton copied the much-corrected type-script onto a computer disk, which I again corrected. I sent a copy to Donald Hall; also to Don Wallis, who by prearrangement tells me what he thinks without worrying about what I think. At various times the manuscript was read by Jack Shoemaker, Trish Hoard, and Rox-anna Font of Shoemaker & Hoard. Julie Wrinn did the copyediting. All these readers matter to me and I care what they think. They make me anxious about my diction, my punctuation, my opinions, my weak-nesses of character. By their reading of this book and previous ones, they have brought me up a niggler, and I am grateful to them all.

I am grateful also to Amy Bentley, whose book, *Eating for Victory,* clarified and improved my memories of rationing during World War II.

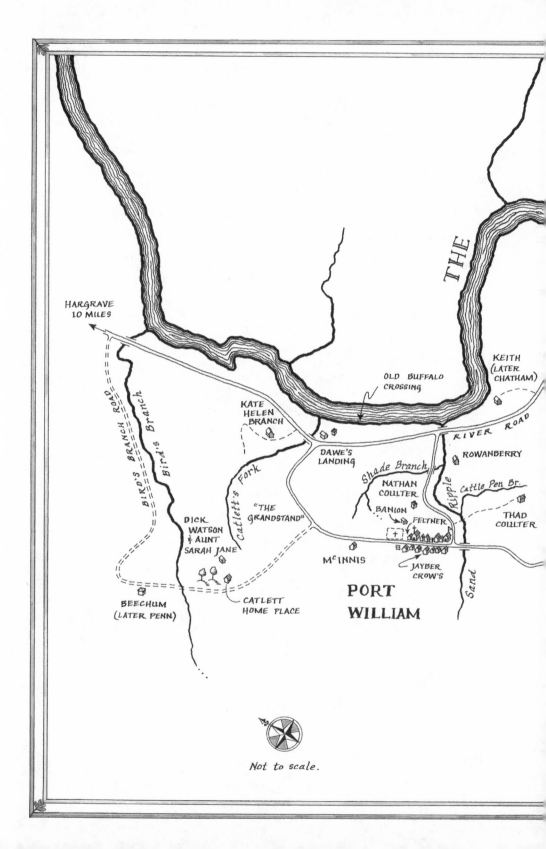

HARGRAVE
10 MILES

THE

KEITH
(LATER
CHATHAM)

OLD BUFFALO
CROSSING

RIVER ROAD

BIRD'S BRANCH ROAD

Bird's Branch

KATE
HELEN
BRANCH

DAWE'S
LANDING

Catlett's Fork

ROWANBERRY

Shade Branch

Cattle Pen Br.

NATHAN
COULTER

Ripple

"THE
GRANDSTAND"

BANION

FELTNER

THAD
COULTER

DICK
WATSON
& AUNT
SARAH JANE

McINNIS

JAYBER
CROW'S

Sand

BEECHUM
(LATER PENN)

CATLETT
HOME PLACE

PORT
WILLIAM

Not to scale.

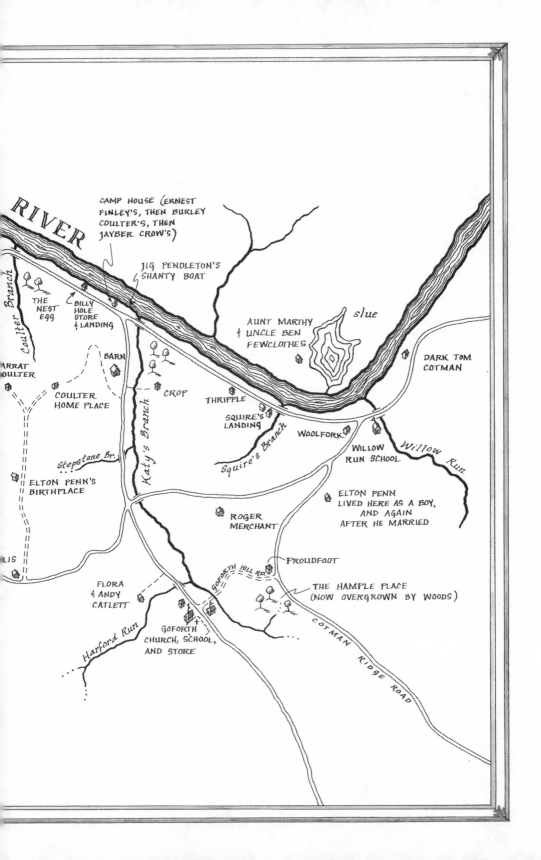

RIVER

CAMP HOUSE (ERNEST
FINLEY'S, THEN BURLEY
COULTER'S, THEN
JAYBER CROW'S)

JIG PENDLETON'S
SHANTY BOAT

Coulter Branch

THE
NEST
EGG

BILLY
HOLE
STORE
& LANDING

AUNT MARTHY
& UNCLE BEN
FEWCLOTHES

slue

DARK TOM
COTMAN

ARRAT
OULTER

BARN

COULTER
HOME PLACE

CROP

THRIPPLE

SQUIRE'S
LANDING

WOOLFORK

WILLOW
RUN SCHOOL

Willow Run

Katy's Branch

Squire's Branch

Stepstone Br.

ELTON PENN'S
BIRTHPLACE

ELTON PENN
LIVED HERE AS A BOY,
AND AGAIN
AFTER HE MARRIED

LIS

ROGER
MERCHANT

PROUDFOOT

GOFORTH HILL RD.

THE HAMPLE PLACE
(NOW OVERGROWN BY WOODS)

FLORA
& ANDY
CATLETT

GOFORTH
CHURCH, SCHOOL,
AND STORE

Harford Run

COTMAN RIDGE ROAD

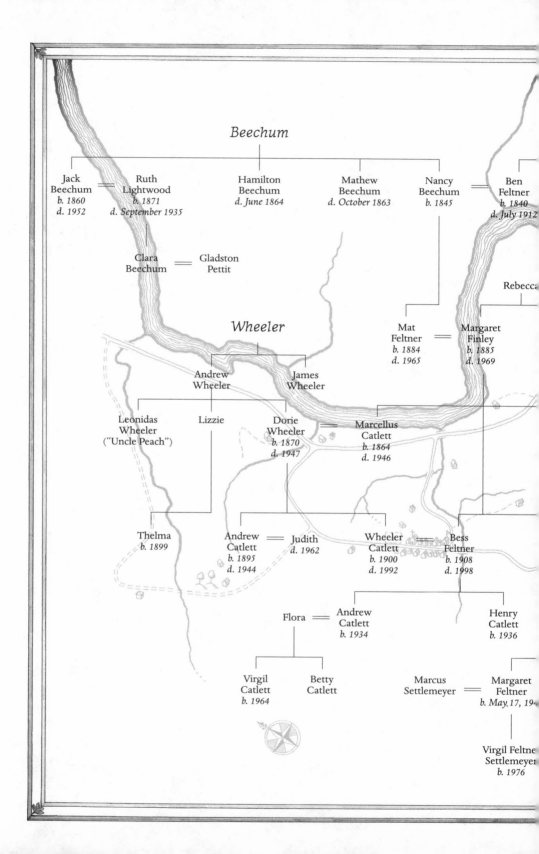

Beechum

Jack
Beechum
b. 1860
d. 1952
═══
Ruth
Lightwood
b. 1871
d. September 1935

Hamilton
Beechum
d. June 1864

Mathew
Beechum
d. October 1863

Nancy
Beechum
b. 1845
═══
Ben
Feltner
b. 1840
d. July 1912

Clara
Beechum
═══
Gladston
Pettit

Rebecca

Wheeler

Mat
Feltner
b. 1884
d. 1965
═══
Margaret
Finley
b. 1885
d. 1969

Andrew
Wheeler

James
Wheeler

Leonidas
Wheeler
("Uncle Peach")

Lizzie

Dorie
Wheeler
b. 1870
d. 1947
═══
Marcellus
Catlett
b. 1864
d. 1946

Thelma
b. 1899

Andrew
Catlett
b. 1895
d. 1944
═══
Judith
d. 1962

Wheeler
Catlett
b. 1900
d. 1992
═══
Bess
Feltner
b. 1908
d. 1998

Flora
═══
Andrew
Catlett
b. 1934

Henry
Catlett
b. 1936

Virgil
Catlett
b. 1964

Betty
Catlett

Marcus
Settlemeyer
═══
Margaret
Feltner
b. May. 17, 194

Virgil Feltne
Settlemeyer
b. 1976

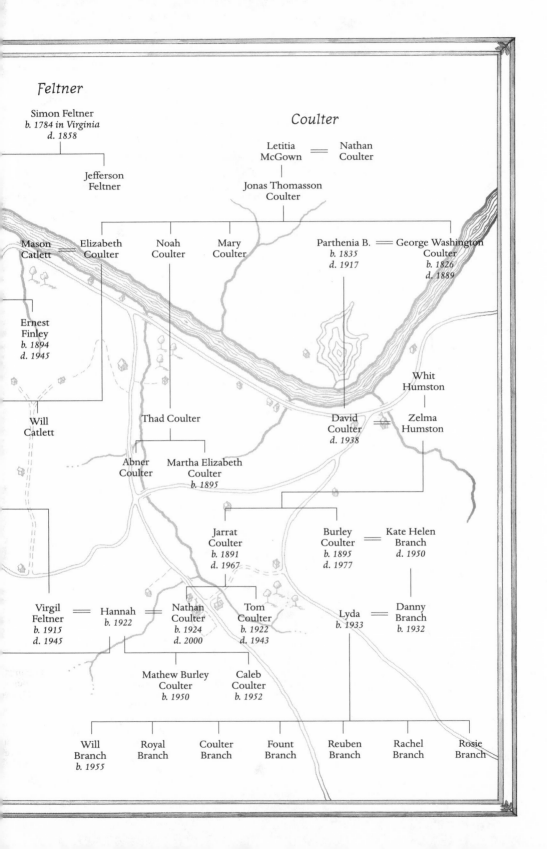

Feltner

Simon Feltner
b. 1784 in Virginia
d. 1858

Jefferson
Feltner

Coulter

Letitia
McGown ═══ Nathan
Coulter

Jonas Thomasson
Coulter

Mason
Catlett ═══ Elizabeth
Coulter   Noah
Coulter   Mary
Coulter

Parthenia B.
b. 1835
d. 1917 ═══ George Washington
Coulter
b. 1826
d. 1889

Ernest
Finley
b. 1894
d. 1945

Whit
Humston

Will
Catlett   Thad Coulter

David
Coulter
d. 1938 ═══ Zelma
Humston

Abner
Coulter   Martha Elizabeth
Coulter
b. 1895

Jarrat
Coulter
b. 1891
d. 1967

Burley
Coulter
b. 1895
d. 1977 ═══ Kate Helen
Branch
d. 1950

Virgil
Feltner
b. 1915
d. 1945 ═══ Hannah
b. 1922 ═══ Nathan
Coulter
b. 1924
d. 2000   Tom
Coulter
b. 1922
d. 1943

Lyda
b. 1933 ═══ Danny
Branch
b. 1932

Mathew Burley
Coulter
b. 1950   Caleb
Coulter
b. 1952

Will
Branch
b. 1955   Royal
Branch   Coulter
Branch   Fount
Branch   Reuben
Branch   Rachel
Branch   Rosie
Branch